Mackenzie smiled. "Babysitting isn't part of your job description. But thank you."

Warmth spread through Justin's chest at her smile. He wondered if he'd ever met a woman he was so blindingly attracted to—and decided in a hurry that was a terrible thought to have about his boss. Definitely a dead end. There was no way on this planet he had any business being attracted to her.

"I'm going to get some coffee. You want a cup?"

"No, thank you. You go on."

He nodded and turned to leave.

But he turned back around to meet her gaze. He started to say that minding her daughters hadn't been work. He'd done it because he'd wanted to. Wanted to make her happy, to help her out.

It was a bad idea to make such a confession.

Dear Reader,

Justin Morant is in a pickle! He's been sent on a mission to Bridesmaids Creek, Texas, and specifically to the Hanging H ranch, where he immediately realizes he's been set up to work for a sexy mama with four tiny daughters at a ranch that was once a celebrated haunted house—not his idea of How to End a Rodeo Career! Falling for the boss lady was never part of the plan, but those little babies are trying to steal his heart. The thing is, maybe his heart was ready to be stolen, because he sure can't imagine life without them, or their spunky, independent mother.

Mackenzie Hawthorne is stunned when the handsome ex-rodeo rider shows up on her porch to apply for the job of ranch foreman. She's not happy when she finds out that her good friend Ty Spurlock has sent the rodeo rebel on a mission of marriage, essentially, but Justin is so sweet with her four babies that soon her heart is in serious danger of falling. She's not interested in marrying again, but Justin seems in no hurry to leave her or the babies—is it possible that this time she's found the man of her dreams?

I invite you to join me in Bridesmaids Creek, Texas, a small town of good-hearted people whose residents have created a man-friendly environment full of legends and so-called magic history to showcase Bridesmaids Creek's many wonderful charms. I hope you'll enjoy this first story, set in a place so mystical it could only be called "home."

All my best,

Tina Leonard

www.TinaLeonard.com
www.Facebook.com/AuthorTinaLeonard
www.Twitter.com/Tina_Leonard

THE REBEL COWBOY'S QUADRUPLETS

—

TINA LEONARD

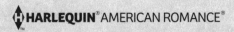

Recycling programs
for this product may
not exist in your area.

ISBN-13: 978-0-373-75526-4

THE REBEL COWBOY'S QUADRUPLETS

Copyright © 2014 by Tina Leonard

Printed in U.S.A.

ABOUT THE AUTHOR

Tina Leonard is a *USA TODAY* bestselling and award-winning author of more than fifty projects, including several popular miniseries for the Harlequin American Romance line. Known for bad-boy heroes and smart, adventurous heroines, her books have made the *USA TODAY,* Waldenbooks, Ingram and Nielsen BookScan bestseller lists. Born on a military base, Tina lived in many states before eventually marrying the boy who did her crayon printing for her in the first grade. You can visit her at www.tinaleonard.com, and follow her on Facebook and Twitter.

Books by Tina Leonard

HARLEQUIN AMERICAN ROMANCE

1241—THE TEXAS RANGER'S TWINS*
1246—THE SECRET AGENT'S SURPRISES*
1250—THE TRIPLETS' RODEO MAN*
1263—THE TEXAS TWINS
1282—THE COWBOY FROM CHRISTMAS PAST
1354—THE COWBOY'S TRIPLETS**
1362—THE COWBOY'S BONUS BABY**
1370—THE BULL RIDER'S TWINS**
1378—HOLIDAY IN A STETSON
      "A Rancho Diablo Christmas"
1385—HIS VALENTINE TRIPLETS**
1393—COWBOY SAM'S QUADRUPLETS**
1401—A CALLAHAN WEDDING**
1411—THE RENEGADE COWBOY RETURNS**
1418—THE COWBOY SOLDIER'S SONS**
1427—CHRISTMAS IN TEXAS
      "Christmas Baby Blessings"
1433—A CALLAHAN OUTLAW'S TWINS**
1445—HIS CALLAHAN BRIDE'S BABY**
1457—BRANDED BY A CALLAHAN**
1465—CALLAHAN COWBOY TRIPLETS**
1473—A CALLAHAN CHRISTMAS MIRACLE**
1481—HER CALLAHAN FAMILY MAN**
1493—SWEET CALLAHAN HOMECOMING**

*The Morgan Men
**Callahan Cowboys

Much love and gratitude to the generous and supportive readers who have embraced my families and communities so enthusiastically—I have the best readers in the world.

Chapter One

Justin Morant recognized trouble when his buddy Ty Spurlock texted him a link to a dating website. This was what happened when you had to leave the rodeo circuit thanks to a career-ending injury: your friends decided you needed a woman with whom to share your retirement, and maybe a spread to call your own because you were going to need something to do with your new spare time. The woman would run your life and the spread would rule your life, and maybe it was one and the same. You'd work hard, be tied to the land and the woman, never have two nickels to call your own. You'd have children and, suddenly, you were up to your neck in obligations and debt.

He'd seen it happen too many times. At twenty-seven, Justin was in no hurry to be fobbed off on a woman who was so desperate for a man that she'd use an online service.

He packed up his duffel, tossed it in his seen-better-days white truck and headed away from Montana, destination unknown, knee killing him this fine summer day.

His phone rang and Justin pulled over. This was a conversation that was going to follow him every step of his self-imposed sabbatical if he didn't stamp it out now.

"I'm not going to answer the ad, Ty," he said, skipping the greetings.

"Hear me out, big guy. I'm *from* Bridesmaids Creek. I know where the Hawthorne spread is. It's the Hanging H ranch, or, as we locals fondly call it, the Haunted H. Go check out the place. You've got nothing better to do, my friend."

"What kind of a name is Haunted H?"

"The Hawthornes used to run a yearly haunted house for kiddies there, and folks remember that. It was bad to the bone, and rug rats to small-fry attended like bees at a hive. Mackenzie's folks did everything they could to turn a dime with it. Her family raked in dough nine months a year with puppet shows, petting zoos, pony rides and lots of good treats."

"Nine months a year?"

"Well, three months a year it was turned into Winter Wonderland at the Haunted H, to go with the town's an-nual Christmastown on the square," Ty said, as if Justin didn't understand the importance of holidays. "You have to appreciate that a haunted house wouldn't be as much of a draw as Santa Claus for the youngsters."

"So what happened to the place?"

"Hard times hit us all, buddy," Ty said, a little myste-riously for Justin's radar. "Give Mackenzie a call. You're burning daylight on this deal. Someone's going to an-swer that ad, which will come as a shock to her because she doesn't know what's been done on her behalf." Ty laughed. "The only thing I haven't been able to figure out is why someone in Bridesmaids Creek hasn't already got-ten her to the altar. I'm not suggesting you try to do that, of course. Small towns usually keep their own pretty well matched up, and judging by her profile on the dating site, that should happen soon enough. Good luck, my friend."

Ty hung up. Justin tossed his Stetson onto the seat with some righteous disgust and pulled back on the road.

He wasn't going to Texas. Not to Bridesmaids Creek to a woman whose family had operated a haunted house.

Just because a man could no longer ride didn't mean he had to make a laughingstock of himself.

MACKENZIE HAWTHORNE SMILED, looking at the four tiny babies finally sleeping in their white bassinets. "Whew," she said to Jade Harper. "Thanks for the help."

"That's what best friends are for." She arranged soft white blankets over each baby, protecting them from the cool drafts blowing from the air conditioner, which seemed to run almost constantly this baking-hot July. "Who would have ever thought Tommy possessed the swimmers to make four beautiful little girls?"

Mackenzie smiled at her adorable daughters, all scrunchy-faced in their tiny pink onesies. "Don't talk to me about my ex. Every time I think about him dating that twenty-year-old, I want to eat chocolate. I'm trying very hard not to do that. Your mother keeps me busy enough with desserts I can't resist."

Jade laughed. "Tommy Fields was never right for you. What you need is a real man." She hugged Mackenzie. "You rest while these little angels are asleep. Mom will be over this afternoon with dinner and to help out. I've got to get down to the peach stand and help make ice cream. 'Bye, darling."

"Thanks for everything."

Jade flopped a hand at her. Mackenzie was grateful for all the friends she had in Bridesmaids Creek. Everyone had been pitching in almost nonstop, bringing food, baby clothes, and giving their time so she could shower and even nap sometimes. She hated to be a burden, but when she mentioned that to anyone, she was reminded that she gave generously of her time to the community, as had her parents.

Mackenzie walked through the huge, heavily ginger-breaded old Victorian mansion, wondering how she was going to fix the fences that were rotting and sagging, not to mention the gutters on the house. Never mind run the horse operation. With four-month-old babies, she was constantly running, taking care of them.

But she wouldn't trade her babies for anything. Tommy might have turned out to be a zero as a husband, but Jade was right: he'd left her with four incredible gifts.

And a lot of bills.

But her parents had been entrepreneurs, smart with money. She had a small cushion, if she was very careful with those funds. She wasn't destitute, thank God. Raising four children was going to take everything she had and then some.

She needed a miracle to keep herself from going into debt, and with no income coming in and no way for her to work until the babies were older, things could get tight fast.

JUSTIN WAS NOBODY'S idea of a miracle, certainly not from his point of view. If the little lady was looking for one, she was doomed to disappointment. Yet here he stood on the porch of the strangest-looking house he'd ever seen two weeks after Ty had tweaked him about it, wondering what in the hell he was thinking by letting his curiosity get the best of him.

The house hovered tall and white on the green hilly land several miles outside Austin. Four tall turrets stretched to the sky, and mullioned windows sparkled on the upper floor. A wide wraparound porch painted sky-blue had a white wicker sofa with blue cushions on it, and a collection of wrought-iron roosters in a clutch near a bristly doormat with a big burgundy *H* on it.

Quaint. The place was homey in a well-worn sort of shabby way, and he'd be sure to tell Ty that he didn't appreciate him sending him out here to see a doll's house in the middle of nowhere. Miles and miles of green pastureland badly in need of mowing surrounded the house, wrapped by white-painted pipe fence so it wasn't totally hopeless, but still. No man would live here willingly.

The door opened, and a petite brunette stared out at him. She didn't come up to his chest, not totally. Brown eyes questioned why he was taking up space on her porch, and he asked himself the same. She was cute as a bunny with sweet features and a curvy body. The matchmaking ad had probably gotten hundreds of interested hits. Not to mention the nice breasts—and as she turned to answer someone who'd asked her something, he noted a seriously lush fanny—yeah, her ad would get hits. He wondered if she knew what Ty had done on her behalf with the dating ad and pulled off his hat, telling himself he'd just introduce himself and go.

This was no place for him.

"Can I help you?"

"I'm looking for Mackenzie Hawthorne. My name's Justin Morant. Ty Spurlock sent me by."

"I'm Mackenzie."

Her voice was as pretty as she was. Justin swallowed. "Ty said you might need some help around here."

Pink lips smiled at him; brown eyes sparkled. He drew back a little, astonished by how darling she was smiling at him like that. Like he was some kind of hero who'd just rolled up on his white steed.

And, damn, he was driving a white truck.

Which was kind of funny if you appreciated irony, and, right now, he felt like he was living it.

Sudden baby wails caught his attention, and hers, too.

"Come on in," she said. "You'll have to excuse me for just a moment. But make yourself at home in the kitchen. There's tea on the counter, and Mrs. Harper's put together a lovely chicken salad. After I feed the babies, we can talk about what kind of work you're looking for. Mrs. Harper will love to pull your life story from you while you eat."

She made fast introductions and then the tiny brunette disappeared, allowing him a better look at that full seat. Blue jeans accentuated the curves, and he figured she was so nicely full-figured because she'd just had a baby.

Damn Ty for pulling this prank on him. His buddy was probably laughing his fool ass off right about now, knowing how Justin felt about settling down and family ties in general. Justin was a loner, at least in spirit. He had lots of friends on the circuit, and he was from a huge family. He had three brothers, all as independent as he was, except for J.T., who liked to stay close to the family and the neighborhood he'd grown up in.

Justin was going to continue to ride alone.

Mrs. Harper smiled at him as he took a barstool at the wide kitchen island. "Welcome, Justin."

"Thank you," he replied, not about to let himself feel welcome. He needed to get out of there as fast as possible. The place was a honey trap of food and good intentions. Another baby wail joined the first, and Justin's ears perked up. Two? Maybe she was babysitting. He looked at Mrs. Harper, worried.

Mrs. Harper laughed. "Yes, she probably does need a hand," she said, misunderstanding the question on his face. "Run on in there and help her out for a second, and I'll serve up a lunch for you that'll take the edge off any hunger pangs you've got." She pulled a fragrant pie from the oven—an apple pie, he guessed—and his stomach rumbled.

Okay, he could go check on the little mother for the price of lunch. But then he was heading out, with a "Sorry—this job doesn't fit the description of my talents," or something equally polite.

He was going to kick Ty's butt hard, over the phone, which wouldn't be nearly as satisfying as doing it in person. He'd driven a day out of his way to apply for what he'd thought might be bona fide employment.

He walked into the den, guided by the baby cries. Mackenzie glanced at him from the sofa. "Don't be scared—they'll calm down in a moment," she said, but he was anyway, unable to stop staring at the four white bassinets, three babies tucked into them like pink-wrapped sausages working free of their casings. Mackenzie held a fourth writhing baby close to her chest, and Justin realized she was nursing.

Holy crap. She had four babies. He backed up a step, belatedly removed his hat. "I'm not scared. I'm something else, but I'm not sure I can identify the emotion." He looked at the three squalling babies, clearly deciding they all wanted their mother's attention at once. "What can I do?"

He hoped she'd say nothing, but instead she pointed him to a bottle. "If you're sincerely asking, Holly's next in line."

Holly? He glanced back at the baskets. Tiny nameplates adorned the bassinets, which for some reason reminded him of the carved beds of the seven dwarves. Only Mackenzie was no Snow White under an evil spell, and he was certainly no handsome prince.

But the lady did need help; that much was clear. She

was in over her head by any reasonable metric, whether it was the ranch (which she probably would lose, if he were a betting man) or these tiny babies (which would require an army of assistants that he figured she couldn't afford—again, no hard bet for a man who liked betting on sure things). This would only take an hour, he figured, and an hour he certainly did have, damn his torn PCL.

Justin studied the nameplates to make certain he picked up the right baby. Holly, Hope, Haven and Heather. All chosen, no doubt, to go with the Hanging H of the ranch, which was sort of a hopeless exercise because they'd all get married one day and their last names would change. To Thomas or Smith or whatever. Then he remembered that Mackenzie's last name was Hawthorne, and she must not have ever changed her name when she got married.

If she'd been married.

Gingerly he picked up Holly, who had a pretty annoyed wail going, grabbed one of the bottles off a wooden tray and slipped it into her mouth. Oh, yeah, that was exactly what she wanted—food—and what he wanted—golden silence.

"Thank you," Mackenzie said. "They all decide they want to eat at once, every time."

He sank onto a sofa, carefully holding the baby. "My brothers and I were the same. It lasted through our teens and drove our parents nuts." He glanced at the other two babies, who were now occupying themselves with listening to the adult voices in the room. "I guess these are all yours."

She smiled, and he noticed she had very shapely lips. He avoided staring at the blanket at her breast, not wanting to catch an accidental glimpse of something he shouldn't see. He was a gentleman, even if he found himself at the moment feeling like a fish out of water.

"They're all mine." She smiled proudly at her children. "We're still working out some things, but the girls are coming along nicely now. They have a little better routine, and the health issues are more manageable."

He turned his gaze back to Holly so the doubt wouldn't show on his face. The overgrown paddocks, the sagging gutters and the chipping paint stayed on his mind. These four children—was the father totally useless? Did he not care about the state of his property? Or these four sweet-faced babies? Not to mention the sexy mother of his children.

"Their father is in Alaska," she said, somehow reading his thoughts. "Working on an oil rig. And when he's not working, he's otherwise engaged. We don't hear from him," she said. "Not before the divorce or after. I'd been on a drug to help me get pregnant, and he was unpleasantly surprised by the results." She put a now-content baby into the empty basket marked "Heather," diapered her, kissed her and picked up Hope. "This one was born with lung issues, but we're slowly getting past that. And Holly has struggled with being underweight, but time has been the healer for that, too." She smiled at Justin, and he saw how beautiful she was, especially when her face lit up as she talked about her children. "So tell me what kind of work you do, and we'll see if our needs match."

He held in a sigh, wondering how to extricate himself from this dilemma. He could help this woman and her brood, but he didn't want to. Justin glanced at the four babies. They had calmed some as they were getting either bottles or a breast—there was a thought he had to stay away from.

Mrs. Harper bustled in with a tray of food for him and took the baby he was holding. "I heard you say that you need to talk business. I'll feed this one, and you eat. Your plates say you're from Montana, so you've come a long way to talk about work. I know you're starved."

No, no, no. He needed a job, but not this job. And the last thing he wanted to do was work for a woman with soft doe eyes and a place that was teetering on becoming unmanageable. From the little he'd seen, there was a lot to do. He had a bum knee and a bad feeling about this. And no desire to be around children.

On the other hand, it couldn't hurt to help out for a week, maybe two, tops. Could it?

He ate a bite of Mrs. Harper's chicken salad, startled by how good it was. Maybe it had been too long since he'd had home cooking. He smelled the wonderful cinnamon aroma of apple pie, and his stomach jumped.

Mackenzie bent over to put the fed, diapered and happy baby she was holding back into the bassinet. He watched her move, looked at her smile, admired her full fanny and breasts—stopped himself cold.

He had no business looking at a new mother. He really had been on the road too long. Glancing around him, Justin took in the soft white-and-blue curtains, the tan sofas, the chairs in a gentle blue-and-white pattern that complemented the drapes. A tan wool rug lay under a blocky coffee table, the edges rounded and perfect for children who would be learning to pull themselves up in a few months.

Taking another bite of Mrs. Harper's delicious meal, he focused on the food and not the homey atmosphere. That's what was wrong: this felt like home. It could draw in a man who wasn't careful, who wasn't aware of the pitfalls.

Maybe Ty hadn't sent him here because of Mackenzie's ad. Maybe she simply needed a grievous amount of help, and Ty had known he needed employment.

He could do this job—or at least he was comfortable with the work he could see that needed to be done.

But he needed to know.

"So about your ad," he said, and Mackenzie and Mrs. Harper looked at him curiously. "On the dating website."

She shook her head. "What dating website? I didn't advertise on a website. I talked to some friends about the position for ranch foreman." She straightened. "Are you saying you came all the way here from Montana because you think I'm looking for a man?"

Chapter Two

Mackenzie planned to give Ty a piece of her mind at the first opportunity. A phone call to express her dismay at his ham-handed matchmaking was tops on her list.

The cowboy who'd clearly been sent on a mercy mission seemed supremely uncomfortable at the outraged question.

"I thought you were looking for help around here," Justin said. "So, yes, I was under the impression you were looking for a man. Though not in the manner in which you may have mistaken."

"Ty put me in a dating website, and you show up here. How would you feel if you were me?"

Mrs. Harper drifted from the room with a baby in her arms. Mackenzie was too upset to cool her temper.

"Probably grateful that one of my friends cared enough to reach out to try to get me some help. Incidentally, I haven't seen the ad. Didn't look." He shrugged, dismissing it.

That was a man for you. It was all about the practicalities, when the mousetrap was perfectly clear to her. You didn't live in Bridesmaids Creek and not know that people plotted to get you married. Always done lovingly in your best interests, of course.

Which was how she'd ended up married the first time—

not that Tommy hadn't been a sinfully gorgeous, totally lazy man more interested in pleasure than anything resembling work.

There was a lot of work to be done around the Hanging H, so named when one of the Hawthorne *H*'s had partially fallen off the sign. The name had stuck—though she knew very well that Daisy Donovan—one of the town's most notorious bad girls—liked to say the ranch was called the Hanging H because the Hawthornes were barely hanging on. Mackenzie did need help, which would have been quite obvious to the handsome cowboy meeting her gaze without hesitation. Tommy might have been handsome in a hedonistic sort of way, but this cowboy had him beat for raw sex appeal.

"You're right. If you're here just for work, and not because of a matchmaking website, I'd like to talk to you more about the position." She decided to give him the benefit of the doubt. Hazel eyes stared at her, unblinking. Justin didn't look like he had romance on the mind. Broad shoulders complemented a trim waist, the sinewy body of a man who spent his time actively. He had a square jaw that hadn't been shaved today—or maybe even yesterday—and shaggy dark hair that hadn't seen a barber in many months.

All in all, the kind of man who would turn women's heads.

"I'd be interested in hearing more about the kind of help you're looking for," he said.

She looked at her babies, tried to turn off the zip of sex appeal that was overruling her ability to think clearly. "Why would you want to work here? There must be a lot of ranches hiring."

He nodded. "I'm sure I can find a job if this doesn't

work out. But Ty seemed to think you could use a foreman."

"A foreman position would be a long-term proposition." She looked at him, curious. "Somehow you don't strike me as a long-term kind of man."

"Things change."

Okay. She'd noticed he had a bit of a limp, and there was probably a story to that. In fact, there was no doubt a story to Justin in general, but she wasn't looking for a colorful background. She needed help here, and the fact was Ty's reference counted for a lot. There was no doubting that Justin didn't want to answer a lot of questions about himself, which was fine because she could ask Ty whatever she wanted to know. She could simply negotiate an open-ended employment offer with Justin.

"Yes, things do change. Thanks for helping out with the babies. If you give me ten minutes to get them settled and grab the books, I'll go over the job requirements with you."

He nodded. "Thanks."

She gazed into his hazel eyes, seeing nothing there but appreciation for a chance of employment. No attraction, no flirtation; just level honesty.

Whatever it was she'd felt from the moment he'd walked into the room, he didn't seem to be affected by it.

Which was fine.

She went to find Mrs. Harper to watch the babies while she talked to Justin. If she hired him, she was going to call Ty.

Whether Mackenzie thanked him or yelled at him about the cowboy in the other room remained to be seen.

Two weeks had gone by, and Mackenzie hadn't seen much of Justin since he'd moved into the foreman's house. But evidence of his presence was obvious: the gutters no longer hung sad and neglected, the paint on the house gleamed, the paddocks were mown and hay was bundled into round bales that studded the landscape outside her window.

It was beginning to look like the Hanging H of old, which brought back a lot of happy memories.

Jade came into the kitchen, peering over her shoulder at the paddocks. "Looks like a postcard, doesn't it?"

Mackenzie nodded. "Maybe I should have thanked Ty for sending Justin my way."

Jade laughed. "You didn't thank him?"

"I was too annoyed when I found out he'd put my name in a dating registry."

"To be fair, that was a tiny fib on his part. He didn't really do that. It was just a little intrigue he threw in for Justin's sake."

Mackenzie shook her head and returned to the babies, who sat in carriers, all four of them, on top of the wide kitchen island. They gazed at different things around the room or their toes, content for the moment. "Ty can get a little crazy at times. But, yes, I should thank him now. The ranch looks like it's in recovery mode."

"And then there's other kinds of recovery," Jade said, still staring out the window. "Is this your daily view?"

Mackenzie turned to see what Jade was goggling at.

Justin. Hot, dark skin gleaming with sweat, bare to his blue-jeaned waist. Muscles for miles. Mackenzie stared at the man wearing a straw Resistol, amazed to feel her heart beating like mad. "Actually, no. That's never been the view."

"Too bad." Jade laughed. "If it was, I'd be eating lunch over here every day with you."

"You do eat lunch with me almost every day. You make the lunch." Mackenzie tore her gaze away from Justin and sat at the island. "I've been meaning to tell you that I feel like things are much more under control. You and your mom don't have to come over here every day anymore to help me out. I'm going to be okay." She smiled at Jade. "You've been amazing friends. You and everybody who's sent food over."

"Pooh," Jade said. "Don't think you're going to run me off now that you've got a bona fide beefcake on the ranch. I'm single, you know."

Mackenzie held Heather's tiny foot in her hand. "By all means, come by if you want to. I just hate to keep taking up your life."

"Believe me—this is a joy and pleasure. And it would kill Mom if you cut off her visiting privileges." Jade stood beside her. "She dotes on these babies. Says they may be the only grandchildren she has because I'm so slow about finding a husband."

"You could try Ty's matchmaking registry."

Jade laughed. "I'll meet my handsome prince when it's meant to be." She went back to staring out the window. "Did you notice his limp?"

Mackenzie sighed. "Yes. It's more pronounced when he doesn't know I'm watching him, which tells me he doesn't want to talk about it. So I don't ask." She tucked the blankets around the babies and smiled. "He does his job. I don't see him. He came into the kitchen last Friday, and I handed him an envelope with his pay in it. Your mother gave him a lunchbox, so I think she's feeding him. That's the relationship we have, and now you know everything I know."

Maybe that would settle Jade's curiosity.

"You have to wonder about that matchmaking story, though. Something brought that handsome stud here. He could have gotten a job where he came from, right?" Jade asked, curiosity clearly not abated.

"Don't ask me. I took Ty's word as a reference and didn't ask too many questions. As you may have noticed, I needed help around here, and if he was looking for a job, I was happy to give him a try." It had nothing to do with the fact that he was, as Jade mentioned, quite handsome. Sexy. Breathtaking, if a woman was looking for a man.

But she wasn't.

"I had a husband," Mackenzie said, looking at her babies with adoring eyes. "And while I wouldn't say I wish I'd never met Tommy—I have him to thank for my sweet children—I can't say a husband is something I'm looking to put on my shopping list. But speaking of shopping, I'm taking you up on your offer to babysit while I go into town to grab some things."

Jade gave up watching Justin and picked up a baby. "I was hoping you were still going to let me babysit. An afternoon out will do you good. And my first-timer's nerves will be calmed."

"You'll do fine! You've helped me almost every day with the babies." Mackenzie hugged her friend.

"My nerves are due to my suspicion that you might not be able to leave your babies for the first time," Jade said, laughing. "Mom's coming by for backup. We have everything under control. Go."

A knock sounded on the kitchen door, and Jade pulled it open. "We don't knock on the back door—just come on in," Jade said, and Justin entered. Even a little sweaty and a bit dirty, he was a sexy, handsome man—just as Jade had noted.

"Ladies," he said, removing his hat.

"Hi," Jade said. She poured him a glass of tea from

the pitcher on the counter. "I'm going to put these babies down for their nap."

She left the room carrying Hope. Mackenzie smiled at Justin as he put the empty glass back on the counter. "Would you like some more?"

"No, thank you."

He had the most amazing eyes, the nicest hands—

Mackenzie pulled her gaze back where it belonged. "The house looks great. And it's nice to see the lawn mowed. Thank you."

He nodded. "I was going to head into town. I figure there's a hardware place and maybe a tractor supply in town so I can get some parts." He glanced at the remaining two babies on the kitchen island after Jade came in and removed Heather. "I thought I'd see if there was anything you need."

Him, maybe? "Thank you. Actually I'm being sent into town myself."

"That's right," Jade said, sailing into the kitchen to pick up Haven, cuddling the baby to her. "It's high time my friend got out. She's a wonderful mother, but everybody needs a break. Although I'll believe that she leaves these babies behind when I see it. Try to help ease her out the door, will you?" She grinned and left.

Justin shrugged. "I can drop you off in town."

Mackenzie hesitated. "That's all right. I can drive."

"I could use a tour."

She looked into his eyes, surprised. "Haven't you been into Bridesmaids Creek?"

"Just ran in to grab some feed for the horses."

There was a lot of lore in Bridesmaids Creek. She was half tempted to go with him so she could tell him all the wonderful stories.

On the other hand, she was tempted to go with him simply because he was the hottest man she'd ever laid eyes on.

Which wasn't the best reason, but it was a reason. She could feel herself melting under his gaze. He seemed so solid, so strong…so unlike Tommy.

"I really—"

"Go," Jade said, coming back into the kitchen to collect the final baby. She cradled Holly as Mrs. Harper came in the back door bearing a pie.

"Hello, everyone," Mrs. Harper said. "I brought something for Justin because I know how much he likes apple pie."

"Yes, ma'am," Justin said. "I can find room for that."

Jade handed Holly to her mother after she put the pie on the counter. "Justin and Mackenzie are just leaving."

"Oh, good," Mrs. Harper said. "That will give me time to make up some fried chicken to go with it for later."

"I think we're not getting any of that pie until we get our chores done," Justin said, his gaze turning to Mackenzie again.

"I think you're right." She also sensed a heavy helping of matchmaking, too, but forewarned was forearmed. She gave Jade a wry look, who returned that with an innocent look. When Justin opened the kitchen door, Mackenzie went out, telling herself that all the matchmaking in the world wasn't going to make her fall in love again.

"After hearing Ty sell Bridesmaids Creek," Justin told Mackenzie as he drove into town, "I'm anxious to get the tour. Ty brags about the Bridesmaids Creek swim, he talks about the Best Man's Fork, and a few other bits of lore, but I was never sure if he was just pulling my leg or not. Ty likes to hear himself talk, and talk big."

"There's a lot of history in BC," Mackenzie said. "Some good, some bad. Just like any place, I guess."

He nodded, pulling his truck into a parking spot in the wide-set, clean town square. Families with kids milled in front of the shops, but not as many as one might expect to see if one were in a city.

Still, it felt like a comfortable town where everyone knew each other, celebrated each other's hopes and joys. "The Wedding Diner?" Justin peered at the white restaurant with its pink-and-white-striped awning, big windows and flashing pink Open sign.

"Home cooking, and, if you're interested, Mrs. Chatham will tell your fortune for you."

Justin grunted. "I don't believe in fortune-telling."

"Oh, she doesn't do read-your-palm kind of stuff. Mrs. Chatham has a completely different method." She got out of the truck and he followed suit, meeting her on the pavement.

"So, shall we meet back here at four?" Mackenzie asked. "I know you said you wanted to go to the feed store. By the way, Ralph Chatham, Jane Chatham's husband, runs that."

"Does he tell fortunes, too?" Justin asked, telling himself to relax and enjoy the small-town ambience.

"Not exactly. But he does do a Magic 8 Ball kind of thing where you pay a small fee, his steer drops a cowpat on a square for you and you win a prize. Or you can trade the prize for one of Mrs. Chatham's sessions."

Justin laughed. "Cow-pie-drop contests are done in lots of places."

"You laugh," Mackenzie said, "but Mr. Chatham's steer is well loved in this town. The steer's name is Target thanks to his aim and the fact that he's made some folks a good bundle of money. Target always hits a mark.

See you at four." She smiled and walked away, stunning him when she walked into a shop with a bouquet-shaped shingle that read "Monsieur Unmatchmaker. Premier Unmatchmaking Service."

Was the whole town backward? Off its collective rocker?

It was none of his business why Mackenzie would need an unmatchmaking service. *Ugh.*

The unforgiving rodeo circuit had been more sane than this town.

Still, he'd been serious about getting a grand tour from Mackenzie, though she obviously hadn't thought he'd meant it. How better to learn about Bridesmaids Creek than from one of the town's favorite daughters?

He glanced toward the unmatchmaking service, seeing that next door to Monsieur Unmatchmaker's dove-gray-painted shop was a pink store with a cheery window and painted scrolling letters that read, "Madame Matchmaker. Premier Matchmaking Service. Where love comes true."

He laughed out loud, startling some passersby. Suddenly he understood why Ty had worked so hard to sell him on this town: the whole place was set up on gigs. Sleights of hand. Fairy tales. From the rumored special steer with excellent aim to The Wedding Diner with the fortune-teller owner to the matchmaking–unmatchmaking rivals—everybody had a gig.

So did Mackenzie, now that he thought about it. Her parents had run a successful haunted house for years, and, according to the talkative fellow at the feed store, parents from miles around had brought their very young kiddies to enjoy the place. No real spooky stuff was allowed. Just down-home bobbing-for-apples fun. Puppet shows, piñatas, a parade with characters.

Until a local murder near Mackenzie's place had

spooked folks. That year, attendance had gone way down. So far down they'd had to close the haunted house. They'd been virtually bankrupted, or so the story went.

"You still here?" Mackenzie asked, shaking him out of his reverie.

He snapped his gaze to hers. "Yeah. Your errand was fast."

Mackenzie nodded. "I just wanted to check in on Monsieur Lafleur. He had gall bladder surgery recently."

"Rough."

"It was rough." She started walking and he followed, more out of a desire to be with her than to hear about Mr. Lafleur's funky gall bladder. "It was gangrenous and they couldn't get to it laparoscopically, so they had to do it the old-fashioned way. Not much fun."

He felt a little sympathy for Mr. Lafleur after all.

"But his wife is wonderful and she took good care of him. They bicker like crazy, but they've been married for fifty years and love blooms in spite of the bickering." She looked up at him, and Justin felt something hit him somewhere near his gall bladder—not his heart—that felt suspiciously like something bordering on attraction.

All this talk of wonky gall bladders was stirring up his desire to eat. That was all it was. He glanced toward The Wedding Diner, wondering if it was safe to go inside and eat without prognostications of marital bliss being preached at him.

"Madame Lafleur runs the matchmaking service," Mackenzie said, snapping his attention back to her and away from the people filing inside the diner.

"The Lafleurs run rival businesses?"

"Complementary businesses. Some people want love, and some people want relationships ended. Monsieur Lafleur doesn't get as many clients as his wife, of course, so he teaches French at the high school and tutors privately in his shop."

"If the divorce rate is around fifty percent, how is it that Monsieur Lafleur has to supplement with teaching and tutoring and his wife doesn't?"

"Because this is Bridesmaids Creek. When matchmaking occurs here—and it occurs often—the relationships tend to stick. Madame Lafleur takes great pride in her ability to bring people together who are perfect soul mates."

He idly wondered if Mackenzie had utilized the services of Madame Lafleur. If so, she didn't seem bothered by the irony of her marriage not lasting. He looked away for a moment, trying to shake off the charm of the town. His rational side said it was just all so ludicrous, and the first chance he got he was going to tell Ty that he'd sent him to a place where people were clearly just one car short of a crazy train.

"Can I buy you a snack? Seems a shame not to take my boss to get a soda and a slice of pie, or whatever is served in The Wedding Diner."

"Sure." She looked at him curiously. "You realize you'll be setting yourself up for the gossip mill."

"Putting myself right in the line of fire." He opened the door for her. "After you."

Chapter Three

Mackenzie and Justin were greeted warmly by the proprietress of The Wedding Diner, an amply shaped woman with a big smile.

"Jane Chatham," Mackenzie said, "I'd like to introduce you to Justin Morant. He's been helping out at my place."

Jane's smile widened as she swept them over to a bright white booth inside the diner. "Welcome, Justin. Those four darlings running you off your boots over there?"

He removed his hat and took the seat she indicated. "It's a nice place."

"Sure it is." Jane laughed. She looked at Mackenzie with a fond smile. "I'm sure you're happy for the help."

"You have no idea."

Justin felt a slow warmth steal up the back of his neck. It was just a job like any job. He rubbed his knee surreptitiously under the table, glad it wasn't aching much today. It wouldn't matter if Mackenzie had twelve kids—he was glad for the work.

And the chance to work for himself. Under a blue sky with no one talking to him.

"Still thinking about selling the place?" Jane asked Mackenzie, and Justin listened hard in spite of himself.

"We'll see what happens," Mackenzie murmured. "In the meantime, can we talk you out of some of that delicious pie I smell?" She looked at Justin, and he felt a tiny zap hit him around his chest cavity again. Really weird, because he'd never been much of a heartburn sufferer.

He told himself he'd grab some antacids later.

"You order what you like," Mackenzie told him, "but I'm not about to pass up that blackberry pie."

"I'll have a slice."

"Two, please," Mackenzie said, and Jane ambled off with a pleased nod.

"You didn't mention you were selling your ranch," Justin said, so startled by the news he forgot he'd intended to mind his own business.

She nodded. "It would probably be best. It's hard for me to keep up with on my own, to be honest, and since I'm not working, I need to keep my savings for my daughters." She smiled. "Selling the Hanging H would mean college educations and a few other things comfortably. I'd like to not stay awake at night worrying about money."

He cleared his throat. "Your ex doesn't pay any child support?"

She shook her head. "Hard to squeeze blood out of a turnip, especially a turnip that stays on the move to avoid child support."

Ouch. Justin sipped the coffee Jane brought over, glad for the dark steaming brew. He then busied himself with the flaky, rich blackberry pie, delicious enough to draw a sigh of pleasure from him if he weren't so caught by Mackenzie's story.

Her plans made total sense. A woman with four brand-new babies, who'd been born with some challenges, was going to need cash. A lot of cash. She was being wise, had clearly given her situation a lot of thought. It was what he'd do were he in her boots.

Seemed a shame to sell a family home, though. He

thought about his childhood home, and how much it had hurt when it was gone. He and his rowdy brothers had grown up there, enjoyed the benefits of living and working on a family ranch. When his father had taken up with another woman, scandalizing the town, his mother had booted him out of the house and sold the family ranch—her right as it was the home she'd grown up in. Though his father had tried to make amends, Dana Morant was made of sterner stuff. She'd taken her boys to Montana to be near her sister, and life had changed forever. Mainly for the better but always with the lingering shadows of what might have been. Jensen Morant now lived on a thousand acres of rich Montana ranchland. Justin didn't go near the place.

He looked at Mackenzie's soft hair and gentle smile.

"You were way far away," she said.

He took another bite of pie, sipped his coffee. "Let me know what I can do to help."

"You have already. I can put the ranch on the market now, thanks to the wonderful shape you're getting it in. I really appreciate it."

A sudden pound on his back had him looking over his shoulder. "Ty!"

"Me in the flesh." Ty slapped him on the back again and nodded at Mackenzie. "Jade told me I'd find this devil here."

"I have things to discuss with you, Ty," Mackenzie said, and he grinned.

"You can thank me later for sending you this guy," Ty said.

"That's just it," Mackenzie said. "You really shouldn't have."

"Getting attached to him?" Ty teased, and Justin decided the conversation had gone far enough.

"Join us," Justin said.

"No. No time." Ty looked at him. "I'm in town for one thing and one thing only. And that's to help you back to the rodeo circuit."

Justin frowned. "How am I going to do that? I'm a bit physically challenged at the moment."

"In a different capacity than riding," Ty said. "You and I are going to travel the country recruiting talent."

"Talent for what?" Justin didn't like the idea of that at all. Correction: once upon a time he might have jumped on it enthusiastically. Traveling the country with one of his best buddies, seeing his friends on the rodeo circuit, giving back to the sport he loved so much—dream-come-true stuff.

His gaze slid to Mackenzie, who watched him with gently smiling eyes as she listened to Ty go on and on with his plans. Justin couldn't work up the same excitement.

He felt like he had plenty to do here in Bridesmaids Creek that was important. Mackenzie smiled at him, a slow, sweet smile. Her big eyes were looking at him, so trusting, and that heartburn he'd been experiencing felt more like his heart was melting into a big soupy puddle.

Dang. This was new. Different.

Maybe hitting the road with Ty was the right idea.

He looked at his friend. "Why don't you stop by the house later and tell me about this harebrained plan of yours?"

Ty looked at Mackenzie. "Would you mind? I know you've got a lot going on over there."

"You're welcome anytime." Mackenzie got up. "Just know that if you take my cowboy, who has become indispensable to me, I'm going to offer you up as a candidate for the Best Man's Fork run. All in the name of charity, of course." She winked at Justin. "I'm going to talk to Jane for a moment."

She headed toward Jane at the cash register. Ty studied his friend.

"You've got the strangest look on your face," Ty said as Justin returned his gaze to Mackenzie. He just couldn't seem to get enough of looking at her. "I'd say you have indigestion, except you're smiling."

Justin relaxed his mouth so the smile would disappear. He *had* been smiling, because his muscles ached a bit. Like he'd been smiling a long time—watching Mackenzie walk and chatter with some friends who came over to talk to her.

"I'm not smiling, but I may have indigestion."

Ty snorted. "I see what's going on here."

"Do you." He made the comment as flat as possible. His buddy's opinion didn't really matter. Ty had no idea what was going on, because Justin had no idea.

"You're tired," Ty said. "Being around those babies and that falling-down farm has worn you out. You better hit the road with me. You'll be back to your old self in no time."

"What was my old self?"

Ty put his hat on, prepared to leave, which was fine with Justin. Then he could go back to surreptitiously staring at Mackenzie. "Grumpy, cranky, annoying."

Justin grunted. "Thought that was you."

"Not me." He peered at Justin. "I really hope this wasn't too much for you, old buddy. I didn't mean to bring you down. Figured some time in a small town with a real job would do you good."

Justin put his hat on, too, because if he didn't get out of there, people were going to notice that he couldn't stop staring at his beautiful boss. "That's what you get for thinking. See you at the house. Don't get there too soon. I'm taking the boss lady shopping."

Ty stared at him, stunned. "What's happened to you?" he whispered. "You're a shadow of your former self!"

Well, that was a question he didn't care to ponder too much. Mackenzie came to stand beside him, smiling up into his face, and his poor stupid heart felt like it took the final dive into his stomach.

What had happened to him, indeed.

Mackenzie and four babies were happening to him, and they were going to require a great deal of consideration. This was a bad idea, this tiny woman with the big eyes and her sweet family. A very bad idea, because he wasn't a family man; he wasn't a staying man.

"You ready?" he asked Mackenzie, and she nodded.

"If you're not going to chicken out," she teased.

Oh, he might. He was thinking about it. Thinking about it hard.

But something told him he probably wouldn't.

FOUR HOURS LATER, when Ty stopped by the house, Mackenzie wondered what her old friend was really up to. Ty had sent Justin to her, now he wanted him to hit the road?

It all seemed very convenient. As if Justin might have conned his buddy into helping him escape the Hanging H with a good reason.

"Anyway," Ty said as the three of them sat at the wide wooden kitchen table, "the reason I stopped by is to get a game plan going with Mackenzie."

"Game plan?" Mackenzie glanced at Justin. If Justin had been part of Ty's game plan, she wasn't sure she wanted to know what the next play was.

"I wouldn't leave you here without backup," Ty said. "I know that in spite of his knee—"

"My knee's fine," Justin said, clearly annoyed.

Mackenzie glanced at him. Occasionally she saw Justin favor his knee, but it did seem as if he'd been limping less since he'd arrived at the Hanging H. The doctor in town had given him a soft knee brace, which he wore without hesitation. Now there were days when Justin walked like he wasn't in any discomfort at all.

"I know your knee's getting better," Ty said. "I'm just saying that in spite of your knee, you've been a big help here. I can see a lot of improvement." Ty shook his head. "Still, I wouldn't leave Mackenzie in the lurch, so I was wondering if you mind, Mackenzie, if I swap cowboys on you."

Mackenzie hesitated. "Swap cowboys?"

"Replace Justin, in a manner of speaking," Ty said. His words ceased entirely when the kitchen door opened and Jade walked in.

"Howdy," Ty said. He stood up to greet the tall, sexy redhead, removing his hat for a moment. "Jade Harper, long time, no see…and clearly I've been missing out."

Jade laughed. "No sweet talk from you, Ty." She gave him a hug and he might have tried to pinch her bottom, but Jade was too fast for him. "Hi, Justin. Mackenzie, who are the three hunky guys who just pulled up in the black truck outside?"

Mackenzie got up to look out the window.

"*That's* the game plan," Ty said with a glance at Justin. "I don't want you to miss my buddy Justin when I take him with me, so I thought I'd trade you, three for one."

"Wow," Jade said. "Grab this deal, is my advice, Mackenzie." She laughed at Justin's smirk.

"Ty, I don't know if I need three—" Mackenzie began.

"You need help out here," Ty said.

Justin didn't say anything, and a bit of unease began

to hit Mackenzie. Did he want to leave? Maybe he'd told Ty that he wanted to. She looked at his face, hazel eyes giving away nothing, his dark hair awry as he ran a hand through it. He looked distinctly uncomfortable.

As Ty had noted, Justin's knee was better—not well enough to ride or run a fast race, maybe, but better—and the last place he wanted to be was stuck here with her and four little baby girls.

"I'll get that," Mackenzie said when knocking erupted on the front door. "Might as well give the candidates a grand tour, let them know what they're getting themselves into."

Justin glanced at her, his eyes widening like he was surprised by her comment. She went through the den, checking the babies quickly—still sound asleep, as was Mrs. Harper in the corner chair—and opened the front door.

Whoa. So much testosterone, so many muscles. "Hi," Mackenzie said, a little startled by all the masculinity crowded on the front porch.

They took off their hats.

"Ty sent us," the tallest one said with a rascally grin. "He said the Haunted H was looking for help to get ready for the county's biggest haunted house and pumpkin patch for miles around."

Mackenzie blinked. What had Ty meant by that? She was selling the place, not going back into business.

"Hello, fellows," Justin said from behind her. "If you're looking for Ty, you'll find him in the side paddock."

"Thanks."

They tipped their hats to Mackenzie and left the porch. Mackenzie turned to look at Justin.

"I don't want to get in the middle of things," Justin said, "but if you want me to leave, just say the word."

"I don't want you to leave." That was the last thing she wanted. "Do you want to go?"

"No. Not if you don't want me to." He shrugged as if he could go either way, whatever she decided. Still, she had the feeling her answers mattered. "I'm not going to say that I know everything about your town or your ranch. But so far things have been working pretty smooth. Or at least I thought they were."

"Ty seems to think he needs you with him." Mackenzie stepped off the porch.

"I'll make that decision." Justin followed her. "Or you will."

Something about this whole thing felt like a setup. Ty's story to the three hunks who'd come riding into town in their big black pickup, that she needed to restart the old family business, felt fishy. Never had she mentioned breathing life back into the haunted house to anyone. It was a dream she'd kept buried, knowing it wasn't practical. She couldn't run that kind of people-intensive business herself, and especially not with four newborns. The small remaining funds she had needed to go into their care—not the vague hope of bringing back the Haunted H.

And yet she had to admit restoring all her family traditions would be a wonderful way to raise her girls. She had had a storied childhood, full of wonder and magic and fairy tales.

But for a fairy tale, one needed a prince.

She looked at the five men leaning against the corral, studying her, waiting for something, some signal. Big, strong, handsome men. They all had rugged appeal, Justin most of all, in her opinion.

A prince had no reason to stay in Bridesmaids Creek—not unless there was a quest, something to make him stay and fight.

"So, Ty," Mackenzie said slowly as Jade came to put her arm through hers for support, "maybe you'd like to explain why you're offering me three cowboys for the price of the one I've already got?"

Chapter Four

"These fellows here," Ty said, grandly waving his arm to indicate his friends, "go by the names of Sam Barr, Squint Mathison and Frog Grant."

"I'm sorry." Mackenzie stared at the last big man who'd been introduced. He was a broad-shouldered man with bright blue eyes and a shock of saddle-brown hair that wouldn't lay flat even if he used molasses on it. "Frog?"

The men laughed. "Gets 'em every time," he said, not minding the attention. "That's not my real name."

"We call him Frog because he looks like he's hopping around like a frog on the back of a bronc." Ty slapped the man on the back. "Anyway, he kind of looks like an amphibian, so it fits."

"I don't see any frog about him," Jade said, and silently Mackenzie agreed.

"These gentlemen have come to apply for the position of hanny," Ty said, delighted to have a stage to sell his snake oil from.

"Hanny?" Mackenzie tried not to laugh. "Is that what you call a working hand now?"

"It means, Miss Mackenzie," Squint said, his brown eyes earnest, "that Ty tells us you need hands to work this place and sometimes some occasional babysitting."

"Oh, a *manny*," Jade said.

"No." Ty shook his head. "A manny is a male nanny. These men are hands. They're also willing to help out with Mackenzie's munchkins."

"That wouldn't be necessary—" Mackenzie began, but Ty shook his head.

"These men haven't seen the inside of a home in so long that a little babysitting would make them happy as clams." He looked at his friends. "And they don't have any problems cleaning up stuff."

"Stuff?" Mackenzie echoed.

"Oh," Jade said. "You promised you wouldn't mention what I told you on the phone, Ty."

Mackenzie glanced at Justin, who shrugged, his whole demeanor screaming, *I had nothing to do with this.*

"Baby spit," Ty said helpfully.

"Upchuck," Squint elaborated.

"Hurl," Sam said.

"Giveback," Frog said, and Mackenzie held up a hand.

"Thank you, but I have it under control," she said with a glance at Jade.

Jade looked guilty. "She handles poo just fine. It's the other that gives her a little trouble."

Embarrassment swept Mackenzie. She couldn't meet Justin's gaze, though she could feel him looking at her. "It was tough in the beginning, but I'm fine now. Anyway, I don't need help with my children."

"And I'm not going anywhere," Justin said.

Mackenzie glanced at him. "You don't have to stay if you need to go with Ty. I'll totally understand. But I haven't got a need for three hands, fellows. Sorry."

"Darn," Jade said. "I wish I'd known that all I had to do to get three handsome hunks to show up in their black truck was have babies. I'd have given that a shot."

The three newcomers seemed to appreciate Jade's comment. Some of the bravado had gone out of them at Mackenzie's refusal of their services, but at Jade's words their air of jauntiness returned.

"You could always give us a free trial," Frog said.

Mackenzie shook her head. "I don't need any help. But come into the kitchen. Let me at least feed you lunch before you go."

"That's an offer I won't refuse," Sam said.

All three gentlemen grouped close around her as she turned to walk to the house.

She looked at them. "I'm okay, guys, really I am."

"You should be resting," Squint said.

"We'll take care of you," Frog told her.

"Guess you're stuck with me, beautiful," Ty told Jade. He put his hand around Jade's arm as they walked.

"I've got some work to do," Justin said, and Mackenzie turned.

"Lunch first. Then you can work all you like." She didn't want him leaving her with Ty. His buddy was working on a plan—maybe big plans—and anyone from Bridesmaids Creek knew that when plans were afoot, you'd better have backup around.

Justin was really handsome backup.

"Sure. I'll come along."

She flashed him a grateful smile. The group went inside, crowding the kitchen, and Mrs. Harper smiled at them.

"Are these the hands Ty was telling me about?" she asked. "I'm Jade's mother, Betty Harper. It'll be nice having more help around here. Now sit down and eat before Mackenzie puts you to work."

Mackenzie started to say that she wasn't hiring anyone, but Jade gave her arm a light pinch.

"What?" Mackenzie said.

"Don't send them away yet," Jade whispered.

"It's not fair to keep them here when I don't have work for them!"

"You have work for them. You could hire a dozen of them and it wouldn't be enough."

Mackenzie looked at the five strong, large men sucking down huge quantities of food. "If I hire these hannies— really harebrained idea of Ty's, by the way—I'd have to pay them. And that's not in my budget."

"We'll figure something out. An idea will come to you," Jade said, comforting her.

"No, it won't." She went into the den to check on her babies, who were all asleep except Hope, who was gazing at the mobile over her playpen. Mackenzie picked her up. "If I had spare money, I'd be putting it away for college educations. Besides, I'm selling the Hanging H."

"Don't be so hasty." Jade took Hope from her. "Give Justin and Ty a chance to help you."

Mackenzie watched as Mrs. Harper fed the big men seated on the wooden barstools around the island. Her gaze wandered to Justin. "If I thought there was a way, I might give it a shot."

"You don't want to get rid of the family home, do you? Wouldn't you like the girls to grow up here?"

"It's just me and four babies," Mackenzie said. "I have to be practical. My folks were a team, and they only had me for many years before my sister was born. My focus needs to be on my children, not running a business and a ranch." She knew from experience that good times could be few and far between when it came to running what amounted to an amusement park.

"You're overlooking one small detail," Jade said. "According to Ty—"

"And that reminds me, you seem to be getting chatty with Ty."

"Not chatty. We talked once. I let slip about the baby spit-up bothering you. Sorry about that."

"I'm past that now," Mackenzie said. "I don't get queasy anymore. I think it just scared me because Hope did it so often."

"The thing you might not be aware of is that these men are looking for a place to stay," Jade said, glancing at the muscled hunks at the kitchen island. "Ty told them they had to pay rent. You'd essentially be a landlord. In other words, money coming in right away. They'd throw in some ranch work, some babysitting, for their meals."

Mackenzie looked at her. "Why is Ty so involved in my business?"

"He says you need help. He needs help. *They* need help." Jade went to the counter, then returned with two pieces of pumpkin spice cake in one hand and a baby in the other arm. She handed a plate to Mackenzie. "Ty says that if you sell, some developer is going to grab this place and cut it up into tiny lots for houses. I'm pretty sure he's right. You're sitting on five hundred acres, Mackenzie. If each house is put even on a large one-acre lot, that's five hundred homes. A thousand homes if they built smaller."

"Is that a bad thing? More housing for Bridesmaids Creek?" She got the image Jade was trying to draw.

"Not necessarily. You think about whether that's what you think should happen in our small, friendly community."

"We don't know that would happen." Mackenzie took a bite of the cake. As always, Mrs. Harper's cake was scrumptious. "The land might go to a hospital, or we could use a new elementary school. Something more beneficial than the Retirement Home for Beat-Up Riders Ty seems to have in mind." She studied the cowboys. Fit, handsome, hunky. But definitely not young enough to keep up on the circuit. And that's what this was really all about. "Justin says he's not going anywhere. So this is all really moot. I don't need help with the babies, and I don't need any more help than Justin." If he was planning on staying.

"Are you counting on him too much?" Jade asked.

Her gaze slid to Justin. She was startled to find his eyes on her. "I don't know," she murmured. "Maybe."

Jade had a good point. It was a mistake to count too much on another person. Witness her ex. She couldn't allow herself to get overly comfortable again.

She heard a motorcycle roar outside, glanced at Ty. Was he having yet another buddy come by? She looked at the cowboys having a great time eating Mrs. Harper's food and regaling her with rodeo stories. Maybe one couldn't have too much of a good thing.

A knock on the paned window of the back door sounded above the laughter. Jade opened the door and Daisy Donovan sashayed in, long brown hair spilling from her helmet, short black leather skirt swinging, black cowboy boots showing off shapely legs even Mackenzie had to admire.

Daisy Donovan had always had radar for hot guys.

"Hello, fellows," Daisy practically cooed. She basked in the sudden stares from the hunks. Ty's buddies had ceased eating, ceased talking and maybe ceased breathing, stunned by the wild-child vision that was Daisy Donovan.

"I brought you a baby gift, Mackenzie," she said, handing her a pink-and-silver wrapped box she pulled from the band of her skirt. The men's gazes never left her. "Hello, Mrs. Harper. Jade."

The guys jumped off their stools to allow Daisy to sit. She smiled and went to stand beside Justin. "I'd love a piece of your delicious cake, Mrs. Harper," Daisy said, her eyes on Justin. She then made certain every man in the room got the full benefit of her smile. Mackenzie was astonished that they all didn't faint from the feminine firepower launched at them.

"Thank you for the gift, Daisy," Mackenzie said. She unwrapped it to find four engraved silver teething rings. A very nice gift, indeed—for a woman who had never really been her friend. Daisy was a natural-born competitor for the male eye, and guys adored her.

"It's just a little something for those sweet babies of yours," Daisy said, smiling at the men. She took a bite of her cake, Marilyn Monroe–sexy, and Mackenzie imagined she heard hearts popping in the kitchen.

"Wonder what the Diva of Destruction wants?" Jade muttered under her breath.

The answer to that was obvious. Daisy was manhunting. And by the looks of how she was staking her claim, she appeared to be hunting Justin.

Mackenzie told herself it didn't matter if Daisy was hunting Justin or not.

She didn't quite convince herself.

"WHAT ARE YOU up to, buddy?" Justin had managed to catch Ty in an unguarded moment in the barn, where he was showing the three new guys the layout of the Hanging H. "It's time you share the plans that are buzzing around in that brain of yours."

"The plans are for you and me to hit the road," Ty said, giving him a genial thump on the back. "I told you—we're going to hunt up recruits."

"Yeah, but you didn't say what we're going to be recruiting talent for." Justin glanced toward Sam, Squint and Frog. "Did those guys make your recruitment list?"

Ty laughed. "Them? No way. They're just replacing

you, which I think is fair, considering I brought you here. I couldn't leave Mackenzie without help."

Justin leaned against a post, crossed his arms. "Why are you so interested in Mackenzie's welfare?"

"It's not just her. It's you, too. And Bridesmaids Creek, if you really want to know."

"You're trying to bring men into Bridesmaids Creek." Justin shook his head. "They have a matchmaker here, you know. Aren't you kind of bumping the competition?"

"Just giving the matchmaker some material to work with."

"Why?" Justin's curiosity was getting the best of him.

"You'd had to have grown up here to understand." Ty shrugged. "The Haunted H was a great draw. Lots of jobs were lost when the Hawthornes had to close it down."

"That's what this is all about? Bringing jobs back to your hometown?"

"Not exactly." Ty wouldn't meet his gaze.

"Oh, I get it." Justin thought he suddenly saw into the cracks of his buddy's mercurial brain. "You're trying to find a man for *Mackenzie.*"

Ty shrugged. "It's complicated."

"Not that complicated." Justin snorted. "When did you decide to play guardian angel to Mackenzie?"

"Since I was the guy with the not-too-swift idea of setting her up with her ex. My onetime good buddy, who turned out to be a weasel of epic proportions."

Justin stared at his friend. "Have you ever considered that maybe Mackenzie doesn't want another husband?"

Ty snorted. "Don't be silly. She's a woman. A woman needs a husband to feel complete."

"I'm not sure I ever saw this chauvinistic side of you before."

"Yes, you did. You just didn't recognize it, because

you and I were thinking alike." Ty laughed. "Don't worry, good buddy. I'm not including you in my plan. Just the opposite. I'm clearing you out to make room for some cowboys who don't wear the rebel badge as enthusiastically as you do."

If being a hard-baked bachelor earned him that honor, he supposed he'd go with the rebel badge. "And that's why I'm being dragged on a recruiting tour? You want me out of the way so your matchmaking has a better chance of succeeding?"

"Look. The idea came to me after I'd sent you here." Ty looked at him patiently. "I realized that Mackenzie didn't just need help bringing back the old place—she needs a husband and a father to those children. I'm the man who fixed her up with the loser, so I'm going to put it right."

"Why don't you just put your own neck into the marriage noose and save everybody some agony if you feel so guilt-ridden?"

Ty put up his hands as if to ward off the very idea. "My conscience is guilty but not stupid."

Justin stared at his friend. It was true. Ty wasn't husband material.

Neither was he.

Justin sighed heavily. "I think you're nuts. But whatever. It's not my town. Nor are these my friends."

Ty brightened. "So you'll do it? The lead stallion agrees to head off and leave the pen to the lesser junior stallions?"

"You make it sound like Mackenzie's ever looked my way twice in a romantic way, which I can assure you she hasn't. We haven't spoken that much since I've been here."

"Call it a hunch. Clearing out the pen, as they say. The ladies always want the one they can't have. Mysterious types seem romantic. Like Zorro."

Justin shrugged. "I think you took one too many falls

off the mechanical bull, Ty, but whatever. I'll go with you," he said, "but you better hope Mackenzie never finds out what you're up to. I have the feeling that little lady doesn't think she needs any man to rescue her."

"Mechanical bull! I was no dime-store cowboy," Ty said, following Justin as he headed back to work. Justin couldn't stand around examining the holes in his friend's head any longer. Mackenzie hadn't given one signal that she might be interested in him in more than a foreman–boss lady relationship.

Still, he had a slightly uneasy feeling about leaving her to the romancing of the Three Dating Daddies—a thought that totally brought him up short.

That's what one of those men might become: a dad to Mackenzie's four little girls.

Maybe the most troubling thought of all.

Chapter Five

"You're going to have to keep an eye on Daisy," Jade told her as Mackenzie settled her daughters down for an afternoon nap. Late-day sun filtered through the windows of the family room, twilight just arriving at nearly seven o'clock. Mackenzie loved summer days when there was so much cheery sunshine.

She couldn't be bothered to think about Daisy Donovan.

"I'm not going to keep an eye on Daisy. I don't care what she does."

"You do care. All of Bridesmaids Creek cares. Her and her band of rowdies are bent on making certain this town drops off the map for families. That way Daisy's father can keep buying up the land around here in his quest for mineral rights and selling huge land parcels to the government. Or worse." Jade flopped down onto a flowered sofa, fanning herself. "As our town bad girl, Daisy lives for herself. My guess is she didn't come here today to bring you a gift, but to check out the new foreman. Everyone is town has been chattering about the hot guy you've got working the place."

"It doesn't matter. I'm not even going to think about Daisy's shenanigans. Even if Justin decided to hop on the back of her motorcycle and roar off into the sunset, I wouldn't think about Daisy."

Jade laughed. "Methinks you protest a bit too much. So what did you think about the three new guys?"

"That Ty and I are going to have to talk. The men are welcome to stay here and bunk in the bunkhouse, but I don't know if I have enough work here for three more men."

"Not unless you reopen the haunted house."

"Which I'm not going to do."

"It's August. We have plenty of time until October," Jade said.

"I know. But my only priority right now is my babies. We'll do fine living in a small cottage in town."

"There might be a miracle. You never know." Jade got up to stare out the window. "She bugs me—I swear she does. Why are men always so blinded by Daisy?"

"Because she's beautiful and has a wild streak. There's nothing blinding about it. It's human nature." Mackenzie smiled at her babies. "You girls, however, must promise your mother to grow up to be teachers, nurses and librarians. No motorcycles for you!"

"My goddaughters won't be Daisies," Jade said, laughing. "However, I think Daisy may be about to kiss a frog."

"Not Frog?" Mackenzie hurried to the window. "Poor Frog! Of all of the new cowboys, I'm pretty sure he's the least suited to Daisy's charms."

"Hate to watch a good man fall." Jade walked away from the window. "In fact, I can't look."

"Can't look at what?" Justin asked, entering the room.

Mackenzie glanced over her shoulder, struck again by how handsome Justin was. She'd gotten a little used to him at the Hanging H, even if she wouldn't share that with a soul. Still, if he wanted to move on with Ty, she'd understand. She'd be sorry—but she'd understand. "We're spying."

"I can see that." He joined her at the window, and Mackenzie was shaken by the sudden warmth of proximity. Almost intimate, their arms nearly touching. She smelled spicy cologne and strong male, felt body heat and strange sensations sweep over her.

She was awfully glad it wasn't Justin out there getting far too close to Daisy Donovan's heart-shaped lips.

"I'LL TAKE THE night shift," Justin told Mackenzie as she finished bathing the girls. She put them into soft nighties and touched a towel gently to the light fuzz atop their heads. A little baby oil for the dry spots, and they were like angels ready to be tucked in for the night.

"You don't have to," Mackenzie said. "But thank you, Justin. Babysitting isn't part of your job description."

"I've been thinking about my job description." He carried Hope and Holly down the hall, so Mackenzie picked up Heather and Haven and followed. She watched the big man settle her daughters ever so gently into their white-ruffled cribs. "This business of Ty bringing on hannies for you, for example."

"Ty is nuts, and there'll be no hannies around here, nor mannies. Silliest thing I've ever heard." Mackenzie covered her daughters with light pink blankets and kissed each of them. "Ty doesn't want to bring those cowboys here to help me as much as he's looking for a place for some of his buddies to work. I'll ask around town, see if anybody needs a couple of hands."

"You know I'm leaving with Ty. Probably day after tomorrow."

She felt a slight prick at that news. "Then I'll only need one of the men. Maybe Frog. He seems pretty harmless."

She sighed to herself. And maybe if he were here he'd be less likely to fall into Daisy's clutches.

"Frog, is it?"

"I can't get used to a grown man being called Frog."

"Hiring him on here isn't going to save him from Daisy."

She looked at Justin. "Who says I want to?"

"I know something about the female mind. And I heard you and Jade talking about saving him."

"Jade was talking about it. I personally think Frog can probably take care of himself just fine." She didn't look at Justin directly. Just too much sex appeal, too much closeness.

It was the babies. She loved the way he took care of her daughters, handling them like they were delicate treasures.

He moved a strand of hair away from her face, and she tucked it up into her ponytail. "I should catch a shower while they're down. We've hit the four-hour mark at night now, and I take full advantage of those four hours."

Justin moved away, sat in the rocker. "Go. Get some rest. I'll keep an eye on them."

"There's no need," she said quickly. "The monitor is on, and I'll hear them—"

He waved a hand at her to leave. "You need four hours to yourself. I'll wake you when they start looking for dinner." A smile tugged at his lips. "Better take me up on my offer. Ty's taking me out of here tomorrow or the next day."

"Oh. Okay. Thank you." She backed up slowly, then turned to hurry down the hall. He was actually leaving. She'd always known he would, and yet she'd hoped— Well, it didn't matter what she'd hoped.

The fact was, she'd gotten used to Justin being around. But it was more than that, and she knew it. Something about the big man made her feel safe and protected and happy. They weren't a family, but they'd gotten into a groove that worked, and she'd come to rely on that comfort. Rely on *him*.

Maybe Jade's right with that protesting too much stuff. I've got a major thing going for this cowboy. I was just trying to ignore it because I knew he'd leave one day.

And now it seemed that day had come.

JUSTIN SLEPT OFF and on, dozing in the room with the babies. It was weird how much he found himself enjoying taking care of them. As a man who'd never been interested in having children—not one bit—he was surprised by how Mackenzie's four little daughters tugged on his heartstrings.

He hated the idea of leaving them—all of them. And, somehow, he even hated the idea of Frog staying behind to take his place. Or any of the three men Ty was bringing on to replace him, for that matter.

The only reason he was leaving with Ty was because Ty had brought him here in the first place. He owed it to him out of a sense of brotherhood. Ty wouldn't ask him if he didn't need him. Mackenzie didn't really need him—not like Ty did.

He needed to talk to Ty a bit more, dig into the mission to settle the questions in his mind. But the thing that unsettled his mind the most was how much he hated the idea of three men he didn't know all that well roaming around the Hanging H and falling for Mackenzie and the girls.

Just as he was beginning to fall for them.

Whether he liked it or not, that was the truth. Justin closed his eyes as he rocked in the chair. The tiny nightlight sent a soft glow over the room. An occasional baby snuffle or sigh reached him, the sound somehow comforting and not intimidating at all, not the way he'd thought it would be. During his wilder, crazier rodeo days, the idea of a family had been distinctly unappealing.

Mackenzie was recently divorced. No doubt the last thing she wanted was another man in her life. He couldn't blame her if that was the way she felt.

At dawn, when Betty Harper appeared in the nursery, Justin felt strangely rested. He smiled at Jade's mother. "Good morning."

"Go get some rest. I'll take over from here. Mackenzie said the babies didn't even move last night."

He felt like he hadn't, either. In fact, he couldn't remember the last time he'd felt so relaxed. "I thought I was awake all night. I didn't even realize Mackenzie came in the nursery."

Betty smiled. "I checked on you at five. Everybody was sound asleep, which is a first for the girls. They probably feel comforted with a man's presence around. Babies do that sometimes. You have a nice deep voice with is probably soothing to them."

She disappeared from the room. Justin rose and stretched. Haven peered up at him from her blanket, and he had the uncanny notion that she was watching him. Did babies see anything at this tender age?

"Hello, little one," he said, approaching her crib. Gently he picked her up, held her close. "Good morning to you, too."

He kissed the top of her head, breathed in the sweet baby freshness of her skin, the scent of baby powder.

"Hi," Mackenzie said, her voice soft.

He turned and saw she was wide-awake and looking refreshed. "You're up bright and early."

"I got a lot more sleep than I have since before I became pregnant." She came to take Haven from him, and he smelled an entirely different smell: strawberry shampoo, delicate floral soap, sexy woman.

His heart did one of those funny flip-flops he'd gotten used to feeling around her.

"Thanks for watching them last night." She gazed up at him. "I think I slept so well because I knew you were standing guard."

Oh, boy. There went the heart. "It was no problem. Part of the job."

"Not part of the job I hired you to do." She looked at him funny.

He backed up a step when he realized he was staring at her pink, glossy lips. "It's the job Frog and Fellows are applying for."

"That's Ty's bright idea. And by now, you know Ty can be a bit of a squirrel." She smiled. "Babysitting isn't part of your job description. But thank you."

Warmth expanded in his chest at her smile. He wondered if he'd ever met a woman he was so blindingly attracted to—and decided in a hurry that was a terrible thought to have about his boss. Definitely a dead end. There was no way on this planet he had any business being attracted to her.

"I'm going to get some coffee. You want a cup?"

"No, thank you. You go on."

He nodded and turned to leave.

Turned back around, met her gaze. Started to say that sitting up with her daughters hadn't been work; he hadn't done it because of Frog and Friends. He'd done it because he'd wanted to. Wanted to make her happy, help her out.

But it was a bad idea to make such a confession. No

purpose to it at all, and he didn't do anything unless he knew the purpose.

Shutting his stupid yap tight before it could say weird, mushy things, he left.

Chapter Six

"Hello, handsome," Justin heard as he got out of his truck, which he'd parked right in front of Madame Matchmaker's small shop.

He turned, found Daisy Donovan just about too close for comfort, chest-high, tiny and dangerous. The brunette was dressed in a short denim skirt, brown cowboy boots and a white halter top. She smiled at him mischievously. All the sex appeal being aimed at him had warning bells ringing like mad inside his head.

"Hi, Daisy."

She wound an arm through his. "Where're you heading to?"

He wasn't about to tell her he'd been planning a visit to Madame Matchmaker. The kind of answers he was looking for required discretion. Daisy didn't look like she did discretion very well. "I was planning to grab lunch."

"Mind if I join you? I had some things I wanted to talk to you about."

He did mind—very much. Ty was hitting the road tomorrow and Justin was going with him, so he had a lot to get done. Lunch with Daisy wasn't on the to-do list.

"I'm leaving town tomorrow, so I'm grabbing take-out. Why don't you call the Hanging H and let Mackenzie know what you need, and maybe one of the new guys she's hired can help you out."

Daisy looked up at him, her dark eyes focused. "We need you here in Bridesmaids Creek."

He shook his head. If there was any reason he'd stay, it would be for Mackenzie. The reason he was leaving was Mackenzie—or, more to the point, the feelings he knew he was developing for his boss.

He extracted himself from Daisy's arm. "Bridesmaids Creek survived without me for many years."

He tipped his hat and pushed open the door of The Wedding Diner. It seemed as if every customer turned to stare at him. Conversation halted.

No, he wasn't imagining the stares. He nodded to the room at large and headed to the pink stand where Jane stared at him, too, her bright blue gaze curious.

Justin removed his hat. "If you have a booth open, ma'am, I'd appreciate it."

She nodded and took him to a white booth. He sat, noticing that everyone followed his progress. No one bothered to hide their curiosity. He hoped she'd bring him a cup of hot coffee sooner rather than later. His stomach rumbled. He could have eaten at the ranch—certainly he'd miss the good cooking there.

But today he really felt a need to put some space between him and the babies. And Mackenzie, most of all.

Jane gazed at him intently. "You're not a settling down kind of man."

"No, ma'am."

"But you're happy at the Hanging H."

The way she made statements instead of asking questions—like she already knew everything but was only giving him a chance to confirm her thoughts—forced his thoughts off the coffee he'd been hunting. "I've enjoyed my time out there."

"But you're not a family man."

He looked at her. "I wonder if I can get a cup of coffee, Jane."

She smiled. "You think I'm digging in your business."

"Yes, ma'am."

"That's what we do here. You'll get used to it. We're really pretty harmless here in Bridesmaids Creek." She cocked her head. "You don't need to worry about us matchmaking."

His brows rose. "I don't?"

"No. We're looking for family men in Bridesmaids Creek."

She strode off to get his coffee. Justin ran a finger around his collar.

A woman with pinkish hair piled high on her head slid into his booth. "Jane tell your fortune?"

He shook his head. "I don't think so."

"She just gave you the third degree." She nodded. "She'll tell your fortune to us later." She stuck a hand across the table for him to shake, which he did, slightly out of his element. "I'm Cosette Lafleur."

"Ah. Would you be Madame Matchmaker?" The French name and the pink-frosted hair seemed like a giveaway.

She looked at him closely. "*Absolument.* And you should have come to see me."

"But I'm not looking for a match."

"That's what we hear." She indicated the diner, whose patrons weren't even bothering to disguise their interest in Cosette's interview of him. "So you're leaving."

"Yes. Tomorrow." He looked at the grilled cheese sandwich and tomato soup a young, bouncy waitress with a nose stud put in front of him. "I didn't order this."

"It's what you get. Miss Jane says you're looking peaky and some protein and calcium will set you right." Cosette shrugged. "Nobody really orders. We all get what Jane thinks we need. It works for us. Most of us never get even a cold!"

Great. He had to pick the one place to get away from Mackenzie where he couldn't get away from talking about her and couldn't even order a nice, greasy burger.

"Go ahead. Take a bite. That cheese is County Line cheese, made off a local farm. You'll never taste better."

A grilled cheese sandwich was just bread and cheese. Nothing fancy. He took a bite, not expecting much. "That's good stuff," he said, surprised.

Cosette looked pleased. "So, back to you leaving. It's too bad you have to go, but Ty said he misjudged you."

"Misjudged me?"

"Ty thought you were probably a man looking for a change in your life. A family man in disguise."

That would be odd. He and Ty had never discussed it. "I'm pretty certain I've never misled anyone about the fact that I like life on the road."

"That's the problem, then, isn't it? Expectations?" She beamed. "Ty shouldn't have tried to put you in a position you wouldn't be comfortable with."

"Are you saying that Ty had me hired on at the Hanging H so I'd fall in love with Mackenzie?"

"Or at least the babies. It's very hard not to fall for those little angels." Cosette glanced up, her smile widening. "Hello, Mackenzie."

He started a little, surprised when Mackenzie slid in next to Cosette and hugged her.

"How are you feeling?" Mackenzie asked. "Your stomach virus has gone?"

"All gone. That soup you sent over for me did the trick. Thank you, dear friend."

Justin ate his sandwich, needing strength after everything he'd heard. Ty wouldn't have brought him to Bridesmaids Creek on a matchmaking mission. His buddy wouldn't have hung him out to dry like that.

But there was no denying that the "bait"—if Mackenzie had been Ty's bait—was worthy of any hook. If he were wired a little differently, if he could consider staying in one place with one woman, Mackenzie would be the one.

Whoa. That was a very strange thought.

She looked at him, her smile innocent and carefree, and he wondered why he hadn't seen it before. Apparently all of Bridesmaids Creek had seen it.

His buddy, best friend, old pal Ty had set him up.

It was a blind date without the date. Nothing more than the same service Madame Matchmaker might provide. And now Ty was pulling the plug, because Justin wasn't a settle-down kind of man, and Ty had found three better victims: Sam, Squint and Fish. No—Frog.

A jealous streak ran up his back.

Which was exactly why he had to leave tomorrow.

"It's such a shame Justin has to go," Cosette told Mackenzie. "He was just telling me how much he was going to miss your little girls."

He hadn't said any such thing. Justin's mouth opened to deny the woman's claim; then he realized what a schmuck he'd sound like if he did. So he nodded and spooned his soup a little faster. Maybe if he kept his mouth busy, he'd keep his foot out of it.

Mackenzie looked at him, her expression polite. "Justin has been a big help at the ranch. And with the girls."

Justin swallowed uncomfortably. Why did he feel so guilty? Did Mackenzie know that her friend Ty had tried to set her up? There were few secrets in Bridesmaids Creek. She had to suspect.

Then again, she'd never given him half a signal that she was interested in him. Hadn't put up much of a fuss when Ty had mentioned they were leaving town, had seemed okay with the new hands.

Maybe he should probe that little situation a bit.

"The new guy should work out well at the Hanging H," Justin said a bit gruffly, not completely able to work out the jealous kink he got about Toad. Or whatever the man's name was.

"You mean *guys*," Mackenzie said. "Ty talked me into taking all three of the new hands on."

Good ol' Ty. If one bachelor didn't pan out, Ty had planned for backup. His friend was almost diabolical with his matchmaking.

"I hear through the BC grapevine," Cosette said, "that your sister is coming home tomorrow, Mackenzie."

Sister? He looked at Mackenzie, noticing instantly that she didn't smile, only nodded gravely.

"Yes. Suz will be home."

Good. Then Mackenzie would have more help, and he'd feel less like a heel for running out on her. Wasn't that what he was doing?

"What are you going to do?" Cosette asked in her sweet, lilting, French-accented voice.

Mackenzie shrugged. "It's her home, too. She can always come home to the Hanging H."

"You don't need a fifth child," Cosette said, and Mackenzie stirred the tea she'd poured a half a packet of sugar into and shrugged.

"Maybe she's changed," Mackenzie said.

"How old is your sister?" Justin asked, curious. The ladies' chatting had turned a bit ominous.

"Suz is twenty-three," Mackenzie said.

And Mackenzie was thirty. Not an uncommon age gap between siblings, but it didn't sound like they were entirely close.

Still, Mackenzie's family problems were none of his concern, and as Cosette had pointed out—much to his chagrin—he had no need to worry. He was being dragged off by Ty because he wasn't looking for a family. And family skeletons were one thing he made every effort to avoid.

JUSTIN KEPT HIMSELF from helping put the babies to bed that night, though it was a ritual he enjoyed. He liked the smell of lavender-scented soap and the sweet sounds they made when Mackenzie slipped them into their cribs. They always looked so darling in their little nighties. Strangely enough, although most people wouldn't find four babies peaceful, that was exactly how he felt at night in the nursery.

Peaceful.

He loved watching Mackenzie do her mom thing, too. It was such a soothing sight as she lovingly slipped her daughters off to dreamland.

He was going to miss it. He'd been lucky that she'd allowed him to become part of the nightly ritual. Part of him wished he could stay at the Hanging H, because he sure did like it here.

On the other hand, now that he knew the price of staying, there was no reason to do so.

They left the nursery, the night-lights glowing softly in the wall sockets, the girls conked out from their busy day and all the good loving from their mother.

So he didn't say he would miss the girls—and Mackenzie—though he knew he would.

Mackenzie went into the kitchen, and he followed. Here

was where he usually said good-night every night, another ritual, this one more professional. They put the babies to bed, they walked into the kitchen and he said *sayonara*.

"Thank you for everything," Mackenzie said. "You've been a big help. I'll admit that when Ty sent you here, I had my doubts." She pulled a cake dish toward her. "Betty left the coffee on and a pound cake she baked. You don't want to leave without tasting Betty's pound cake."

He found himself nodding before he even sat down, glad of the excuse to stay. "I'll take you up on that offer. Thanks."

She poured him a steaming mug of coffee he suddenly realized he didn't want. She cut him a fragrant slice of cake he suddenly didn't want, either.

And when Mackenzie passed him to rinse off the knife, he reached out and caught her hand. "I'm going to miss this."

Her face held surprise—then she smiled. "Thank you."

He noticed she didn't take her hand from his, so he did the only thing he could. He set her cake knife on the counter and pulled Mackenzie to him. She stared up at him with those beautiful brown eyes, and he kissed her lips, ever so lightly, just in case she didn't want to be kissed. There was still time to stop before it was a full-blown kiss. He'd know in a second if he'd gone someplace she didn't want him to go.

Mackenzie didn't move—she stayed still as the night, waiting—and Justin was never so glad of anything in his life. He pressed his lips against hers, letting himself sink into the sweetness. He heard rain begin spattering against the windows, but that was the outside world. In this warm, cake-scented kitchen, he held the softest woman in the country in his arms, and she was responding to him.

The back door blew open. Mackenzie and Justin

jumped apart. He stared at the woman in the doorway. She was dripping from her head to her toes, her boots muddy, her jeans ragged and pocked with deliberate tears. She dropped a dirty duffel bag onto the floor. But it was her short pixie hair, blond with blue streaks, that stopped him, not to mention the cheek stud and the dark glaring eyes.

"Suz!" Mackenzie flew to hug her sister, enveloping her.

Suz stared at him over Mackenzie's shoulder. "Who's he?"

"This is Justin Morant." Mackenzie sounded uncomfortable. "He's the foreman. Until tomorrow, that is."

Suz didn't move to shake his hand. Didn't leave her sister's arms.

"What's he doing in the kitchen at this hour?" Suz demanded.

Damn good question. He grabbed his hat, went to the door. "I'll say goodbye tomorrow before I go, Mackenzie."

Suz glared, willing him gone. Mackenzie nodded. "Thank you."

Ouch. He nodded and headed out into the rain, leaving the cake and the coffee behind.

The kiss stayed with him.

Chapter Seven

Justin came upon Frog, Squint and Sam spying on the house from the bunkhouse. "What the hell, fellows?" he demanded.

"Didn't you see her?" Frog asked. "That little bit of darling that roared up on the motorcycle?"

He hadn't seen a motorcycle, hadn't heard one, wouldn't have noticed one if it had run over his foot. All he'd been focused on was Mackenzie in his arms. He didn't think he'd ever forget that.

She was all woman, gentle and sweet-smelling. Curves. Heaven.

No wonder her sister was so protective of her. He would be, too.

"That *darling* is too much for any of you to handle." He hung his hat on the hook and went into the kitchen for a much-needed beer, eschewing the temptation to spy on the kitchen, which faced the bunkhouse.

"Who was she?" Frog asked.

"Little sister. Nothing for you to worry about." Justin flung himself onto the leather sofa.

"I'm not worried about her," Squint said. "If I can't have Mackenzie, I'll be happy to—"

"Whoa, whoa, whoa." Justin scowled at the three

stooges he was stuck with for the moment. "No one said you were getting Mackenzie or Suz."

"Suz," Sam said dreamily. "I could have guessed she had a pretty name."

Justin mentally rolled his eyes. "Again, who said those women were available? You work for them. You can't hit on them."

They looked at him, grinning.

"If you had understood your assignment," Frog said, "you would have known that romancing is what we're all here for. We're all bachelors looking for a good wife and a home."

Justin blinked. "What assignment?"

"Didn't Ty tell you? In this town, the ladies are looking for a husband any way they can find one," Squint said. "And we are all preapproved to join the race to the altar."

"Where did you get a name like Squint?" Ty asked.

"Name's John Squint Mathison," the tall man said. Justin supposed he was a decent-looking fellow, the kind a lady might call a hunk. "I got *Squint* in the military."

"I don't like it," Justin said. "It sounds a bit shady."

"Au contraire," Sam said with a flourish. "If you'd been in the mountains of Afghanistan with us, you'd have wanted this one and his peashooter at your back. We called him Squint-Eye, Squint for short, for certain reasons best not discussed. But you can trust it was a badge of honor."

"Yeah, well." He looked at the gentle giant next to him. "I guess I don't want to know what Frog is derived from," he said, feeling a little sour that these gentlemen would be staying and he'd be going. Gentlemen, indeed. More like woman-hunting, non-commitment-phobic, nice guys.

They shook their heads solemnly, and he sighed.

"What makes Ty so sure that Bridesmaids Creek is so ripe for marriage-hunting males?"

"Did you get a load of that beauty that pulled up on the motorcycle yesterday?" Sam's eyes went round.

"Daisy Donovan? Yes, I did." Justin shrugged.

"She's *fine*. And she invited us all to a special gathering." Frog looked pleased. "I'd marry her in a heartbeat."

From what he'd heard about Daisy, Justin didn't think that was necessarily a good idea. He sipped his beer, studied the eager bachelors in whose capable hands he was leaving Mackenzie.

"Don't worry," Squint said, as if reading his mind. "We'll take care of everything. We've figured out your routine."

They knew what he did outside the house. Inside the house with Mackenzie and the babies, they had no idea.

He'd like to keep it that way.

"I'M SO GLAD you're home, Suz," Mackenzie told her sister when she wandered back into the kitchen, freshly showered and wearing comfortable pajamas. Mackenzie passed her sister the slice of pound cake she'd cut for Justin and made her a hot cup of tea. "How was Africa?"

Suz sat on a barstool and glared at her sister. "Africa was beautiful. I think we did a lot of good with the limited resources we had. We can talk about that later, after I've seen my nieces again. And after we talk about that cowboy you were in here sucking face with."

"I was not," Mackenzie said, placing the teacup in front of her sister and pushing the sugar bowl close, "sucking face with the cowboy."

Suz shook her head. "I do believe if I hadn't walked in, this kitchen would have seen some action."

Mackenzie looked at her little sister with a noncommittal shrug. "I doubt that."

"Do not fall into another man's arms just because what's-his-face went off with what's-her-face."

That familiar sting lodged deep inside her, yet stinging less than it once had. "I am not falling."

Pants on fire. It had been wonderful for the few seconds Justin had held her in his arms. The feeling had shocked her when he'd pulled her close against his broad chest, right up to his hard body. She'd watched him many a time from this kitchen window, admiring the muscles and the quiet, steady, strong way he went about his work. Being held by Justin had sent her heart rushing out of control.

"Oh, no," Suz said, staring at her sister. "I've seen that look on your face before."

"What look?"

"That about-to-fall look."

"I am not about to fall. In fact, Justin's leaving tomorrow. So falling is out of the question."

Suz shook her head, started in on the pound cake. "It's rebound. Surely you know that."

"So what?"

"I mean," Suz said, her mouth full, "if you were the type of woman who would just kiss and quit, that would be one thing. But you kiss and marry. And that's a problem."

Mackenzie laughed. "If you knew Justin, you wouldn't worry. He is so not the marrying kind. Everybody knows that."

"Everybody can't know that, because he was only here a short time." Suz was being practical. "You don't know for sure."

"Regardless, he's leaving tomorrow." She wasn't entirely happy about that, but Ty could be inscrutable about anything and everything. Certainly Justin hadn't argued about leaving.

So it was for the best.

"Anyway," Suz said, sipping her tea, "how are my angel cakes? I peeked in on them, and they were sleeping hard. Haven sucks her thumb, you know. It's cute."

"She doesn't do that when she's awake." Mackenzie smiled. "They're amazing. There's not a day I don't thank Heaven that I have them."

"Yeah, well," Suz said gruffly. "It was the least Knuckle-head could do for you." She sniffed. "You look good."

Mackenzie smiled. "Do I?"

"Yeah. You gained a little weight. You look rested." Suz sniffed again. "In fact, you look beautiful."

Mackenzie stared at her normally unsentimental sister. "Why are you buttering me up?"

Suz laughed. "I'm not. I'm being my typical honest self. Some days it's brutal, and some days it's all good news. You really do look great. I'm sure I'm not the only one who's told you that recently."

"Believe it or not, the cowboy, as you call Justin, and I don't have some hot love affair going. Before today, we hadn't spoken more than twenty minutes at one time."

"I don't think talking's what's on his mind."

"He's been nothing but a gentleman. If you're done with your snack, I'm going to tuck you onto the sofa and turn on the TV. I may look great, but you look like the flight was long."

Her sister followed her from the kitchen. "It was long and hellish. I always say I'm quitting the Peace Corps. But then I don't. I can't. It's in my blood."

Mackenzie settled her sister in her old room, spreading a soft blue-and-white afghan over her that Betty had knitted. Suz had the reputation for being a wild child— she was tough and a little wild. But she had such a good heart. And she'd go places no one else would go, in the quest to do what few others wanted to do. Or could do. She gazed at her sister tenderly. "How long are you here?"

"Not long." Suz's eyes started to close. "Just until I determine that you're not suffering too much without me. And until I make sure you don't do something dumb, like fall for a cowboy with a restless leg."

Mackenzie brushed Suz's blue-streaked hair away from her forehead. "Restless side, darling. Restless leg is something entirely different."

"No, I'm pretty sure I'm worried about his restless leg." Suz's eyes drifted shut. "It's always so good to be home. This will always be our home, won't it?"

Mackenzie felt a pang of guilt. This was a discussion for another day. She patted Suz's hand, noted the cracked nails, the dry skin, the calluses. Suz was a warrior of a different kind, a misunderstood warrior, and Mackenzie would do anything to protect her.

But keeping the family home probably wasn't in the cards. "Rest now."

"I try," Suz said. "I try to rest, Mackenzie. But I always see them."

Mackenzie drew back a little. "Don't think about it. It's all over."

Suz nodded, and Mackenzie tucked the blanket close around her sister, cocooning her like she would one of her babies. Then she went into the kitchen and looked out toward the bunkhouse, staring into the darkness.

Suz was right about one thing—Justin had made it clear he was a footloose, rebellious kind of guy. There was no reason to fall for him. Suz walking in had probably stopped something that should never have been started.

But she was amazed by the feelings his kiss had awakened inside her, feelings she'd never had before. Suz was right. The kitchen table probably would have been used for something other than its intended purpose, because the last thing Mackenzie had wanted was for Justin to let her go.

And that's why it hurt so much that he was leaving.

JUSTIN WAS AWAKENED by the feel of something warm and curvy sliding into bed, curling right up against him. He blinked, realizing he wasn't dreaming.

But something was wrong. For one heavenly second he thought Mackenzie might have crawled into his bed.

The perfume wasn't right. The hands were too greedy. He caught the hands and sat up, switching on the lamp.

"Daisy! What the hell?"

She blinked and hopped out of his bed naked as the day she'd been born. He averted his gaze from the flash of skin as she scooped up her clothes and began dressing. "I thought—"

"You thought what?" He got up, pulled on his jeans, annoyed. There were three other occupants of the bunkhouse. Any one of them would probably have been happy to find Daisy in his bed.

He was not.

"Never mind." Daisy had pulled on some of her clothes but definitely couldn't be called "dressed."

Which of course was when the three stooges entered the room. Their eyes bugged from their sockets.

"This isn't what it looks like," Justin said, zipping his jeans. "She's lost."

The stooges looked concerned.

"Not that lost," Frog said.

"Damn, son," Squint said. "You're exactly what we heard about you."

"Which is what?" Justin demanded.

"Emotionally unavailable," Daisy said, slowly pulling the straps up on her dress. "A real renegade."

Justin hesitated, realizing Daisy was putting on something of an award-worthy act. "What the hell is going on here?"

"Nothing," Sam said, "except that you were in bed with Daisy."

"I was not in bed with Daisy!"

"Someone was in bed with Daisy, and it wasn't us," Frog said. "One of us, I should say," he said; then he was suddenly shoved aside.

Mackenzie stared at him. "What are you doing here, Daisy?"

"Nothing," Daisy said, her voice too sweet. Too silky, a bit catty.

Justin sighed. "Everybody out of my room. Now."

Mackenzie turned to leave, too. "Not you," he said, grabbing her hand and pulling her back into the room. He closed the door, took the lunch sack from her hand and set it on his dresser. "Were you bringing me a snack bag for the road?"

She glared at him. "Yes."

"Bet you'd like to take it back."

"Yes, I would!"

"Well, you can't." He pulled her into his arms, taking her lips with his, kissing her the way he'd wanted to kiss her earlier.

She put her hands on his chest, pushed him slightly away—though not too far. "Why would I want to kiss you after Daisy Donovan's been in your room?"

"Because you're in my room now."

"Which begs the question what was she doing in here?"

He smiled. "I think she'd lost her way."

"I very much doubt it."

"I'm pretty certain I wasn't the intended target. And you sound like you may have a jealous streak, boss lady."

"I'm not jealous in the least. I'm *concerned*."

Now she did try to tug away from him, though he didn't allow that. She didn't try hard enough for it to count—and he was pretty intrigued by this *concerned* side of her. "*I'm* concerned that you don't leave without what you came for," he said, slanting his lips over hers, drawing her in for a deep kiss. He loved holding her, that was for certain; she was soft and, at this moment, a trifle annoyed, which he was going to enjoy kissing right out of her.

Her lips were sweeter than he'd ever imagined. Every kiss, every stroke, was more amazing than before. Mackenzie let out what sounded like a tiny whimper, and he wasn't about to stop now. No longer stiff in his arms, she was pliable and leaning into him, her hands reaching up behind his neck, pulling him closer.

God, he didn't think he could leave this.

The thought brought him right down to earth. He really had no right to be doing this. Not to Mackenzie. If Daisy played fast and loose, Mackenzie was the kind of woman a man didn't play with at all. "Hey," he said, pulling back. He moved away, jerked his head toward the lunch sack. "Thanks for bringing my lunch. I really appreciate it."

She put her hands on her hips. "Chicken much?"

He was—he was a chicken with all the trimmings. "Maybe."

"At least you admit it."

"What else can I do?"

"Whatever you want to."

What he wanted to do was drag her into bed. Make love to her all night long. But what would that solve besides momentarily easing the overwhelming attraction he felt for her? It wasn't fair—he couldn't make love to Mackenzie and then hit the road. Not with those four little babies at the big house who needed a father, not a man who made love to their mother and then disappeared.

"You make things hard, Mackenzie."

She raised a brow. "If anyone's making anything hard for you, it's just you. I only brought you a lunch."

She had him there. He was all kinds of torn up, and he couldn't blame it on her. "I hate the thought of leaving you with the three amigos."

"Why? Ty trusts them."

Justin wasn't certain how much he trusted Ty. Heck, he didn't trust him at all. Ty was running a matchmaking game to get Mackenzie to the altar.

"Maybe I'll stay," he said, the words popping out of his mouth before he'd measured them.

She looked at him a long time. "Whether you stay or go is your decision," she said, disappearing from his room. He heard the front door close and took a deep breath.

I screwed that up every which way from Sunday. Holy cow.

Daisy climbing into his bed had started off a chain reaction. Mackenzie didn't trust him now; he could feel that. Already burned by one man, she had her guard up. It had taken him weeks to get past those shields, and now they were going to be stronger than ever.

He went to find his bunkhouse mates. Daisy was long gone, and Frog, Sam and Squint loafed on the leather sectional.

"Boss lady just blew out of here like a whirlwind," Squint observed. "Guess she didn't like what you were selling."

Ah. Ribbing from the dating-challenged. "If you have a point, make it, fellows."

"No point," Frog said quickly. "Except it seems to us your chips are down."

"And you see an opening?" He leaned against the wall, staring down at them. "Maybe. Maybe not."

Sam grinned at him. "The only maybe is maybe you shouldn't be leaving. Field's going to be wide-open."

"Thanks for the advice." Justin grabbed his lunch, headed to his truck.

The three boneheads followed him out.

"The only reason we're trying to help you is that Daisy says without you, this dump's going down," Squint said. "Kinda hate to see that happen to the little lady. She's got those four tiny whinies, you know."

Justin glanced toward the house. "Are you going to follow me out of town?"

Sam shoved his hands in his pockets. "No. We're going into town to meet Daisy. She wants to show us her place."

Justin turned. "So which one of you was Daisy coming to see this morning when she accidentally got in my bed?"

Frog shook his head. "That was no accident. She was trying to get you in trouble with Mackenzie."

"How do you know that?" It was a very strange thought.

"She left without getting into any of our beds, didn't she?" Squint asked. "Though believe me, we wouldn't have thrown her out of bed for eating crackers."

"I didn't throw her out of bed," Justin said. "I didn't *want* her in my bed." He frowned. "She wouldn't have had any idea that Mackenzie was coming to the bunkhouse to say goodbye. So how do you know it was a setup?"

"It's the way ladies work," Frog said. "At your age, you should know this."

"Daisy sure did disappear once she stirred up trouble," Squint said. "So if Trouble won't come to us, we're going to Trouble."

"But why?" Justin was confused. "Why would you want to bother with a wild woman like Daisy?"

"For many reasons." Sam thumped him jovially on the back. "We shouldn't have to draw you a picture, but one of those reasons involve the benefits you were going to receive this morning."

"Sex?" Justin frowned. "That seems cold-blooded, doesn't it?"

"The world runs on sex," Frog said expansively. "Do you know we get hit with like a bajillion sexual messages a day?"

"It's sort of like subliminal phone calls," Sam said. "Only you don't seem inclined to pick up the phone. So one of us will."

Justin shook his head. "I don't care." He got into his truck.

"Anyway," Squint said, "the real reason we're going to see Daisy is that we consider ourselves something like spies. Spies with muscles and highly desirable—"

"Brains," Frog interrupted. "This is brain warfare. We're not going to let Mackenzie and those little girls down."

Justin's gaze narrowed. "You just said your interest in Daisy is sex."

"All good spies do what they have to do," Squint said. "But the mission is to keep Daisy from sinking Mackenzie. But go on—run off if that's what you were born to do. Born to run and all that. We get it."

"Back up a second," Justin said. "You're going to try to seduce Daisy so she'll tell you what she and her father are up to in their plan to get Mackenzie to sell out? Because apparently this isn't the first rodeo with the Donovan crowd."

"Not seduce, exactly. More like romance," Sam said. "Sweet talk."

"There's just one problem with your plan. Daisy got

into my bed. Not one of yours. What if she's not interested in the bait you're dangling?"

"Well, we figure absence makes the heart go wander. The three of us can convince her you were never here," Frog said.

"Sounds like a plan," Justin said, not wanting to hurt their feelings. "You do know that Mackenzie is planning to sell the Hanging H, don't you?"

"Yes, but Ty says she can't. He says we have to help her. Because Daisy's family will buy it and carve it up into tiny land parcels. And the Hanging H means jobs and commerce when Mackenzie starts the haunted house back up."

"But she doesn't want to," Justin said. "Mackenzie has four babies she's juggling. This plan of yours has so many holes in it that it could be your heads."

"Ty says Mackenzie just needs time. That she's all emotional right now, hormonal and stuff. Worried about the future. But he says that what's good for Bridesmaids Creek is Mackenzie, and what's good for Mackenzie is Bridesmaids Creek. So we're men on a mission, brother."

Justin considered their words, caught by their earnest worry about Mackenzie and her daughters.

"Gives you pause, doesn't it?" Squint asked.

Justin grunted.

"Don't bother him. He's beginning to see the light," Frog whispered. "It's like watching a fire slowly coming to life."

Justin ignored the ribbing. He had to admit the points were salient—*if* he trusted Ty's machinations, *if* he wanted to fall in with men with names like Squint, Frog and Toad—er, Sam. *If* he wanted to spend more time in a place with a crazy, totally female name like Bridesmaids Creek. That would be the address his mail was sent to from now on. Justin Morant, Bridesmaids Creek, Texas. Mr. Badass Bull Rider from Bridesmaids Creek.

"Shall we help you unpack that duffel from your truck for you?" Sam asked.

Justin thought about Mackenzie's sweet lips against his, responding ever so cautiously—and then more warmly as she opened up to him. It had been a helluva rush.

Ty wanted to drag him away from Mackenzie, open the playing field up to more serious contenders. But the little lady had an awful lot of serious warfare being waged against her.

He looked at his three new friends earnestly awaiting his answer.

"Do the right thing," Frog said softly.

What the hell. He got most of his correspondence by email or text anyway. Justin got out of the truck.

He realized Mackenzie and Suz were standing in the driveway not forty yards away. Suz's arms were crossed, her posture belligerent. He had some smoothing over to do with little sister.

But it was Mackenzie he was staying for—and that was something the man he'd been even a week ago wouldn't have ever considered.

Chapter Eight

"I don't need four ranch hands," Mackenzie told Suz as she watched the men return to the bunkhouse. "Frankly, I'm not even sure I want one."

"Looks like you've got them. Maybe it's time to tell Ty his plan's not going to work." Suz sat down on a stool at the kitchen island and pondered a tat on her inner arm Mackenzie hadn't known she'd added to her collection, a tiny heart with the initials *HH* scrolled inside.

Hanging H.

"Would you please quit getting tattoos?" Mackenzie said. "When you get to be a hundred, you're going to be a wrinkled mass of ink."

Suz laughed. "Live for today, sister."

She didn't have that luxury. "Don't you ever want to settle down? Find the right guy?"

"Didn't work for you." Suz brightened. "Although I can tell my nieces are going to be amazing women, with love and direction from their Aunt Suz."

Mackenzie sat across from her sister and reached out to take her hand. "When's your next assignment?"

"I've decided there isn't going to be one. Africa was my last stop." Suz sighed. "Even a rolling stone with a mission has to grow moss sometime."

Mackenzie looked at her sister, worried. "This isn't like you. You never wanted to settle down."

"Dearest sister. I didn't want to settle down before I did something with my life. Now I've done a little." She shrugged, and they both glanced up as the kitchen door opened a crack.

"Can I come in?" Justin asked.

Mackenzie's heart did a funny little skip. "Sure. Have a seat."

"I saw the kitchen light was still on. Figured that meant the coffeepot might still have a few grounds left in it."

"Not really," Suz said.

"Suz!" Mackenzie said.

"Oh, all right." She got up ungraciously to get Justin a mug. "It's not coffee. It's tea at this hour. Can you deal with that?"

Justin smiled. "Sure."

"You want the milk and the sugar and the full deal, or—"

"Just hot. Thanks." Justin sat across from Mackenzie. "I don't think you need four hands."

"I just said that to Suz."

Justin nodded. "The three eligible bachelors have appointed themselves your guardians, courtesy of Ty."

"Told you you're going to have to talk to him," Suz said, setting the mug in front of Justin. "I'm going to bed, kids. Don't do anything I wouldn't do."

"Night, Suz." Mackenzie shook her head. "Wait—come back here!"

Suz turned in the doorway. "Yes, sister dear?"

"Finish the story about your life now that you're done with the Peace Corps."

"Oh. That's easy." Suz grinned. "I'm going to finish

college. I only have two years left. Then I'm applying to medical school." She drifted out of the room, humming.

College. Medical school. Mackenzie ran through the amount of money she had left from their parents' estate.

"Problems?" Justin asked.

"No." She got up to cut them both a piece of pound cake and set one in front of him. "Why did you decide to stay? You didn't have to."

"Yeah, I kind of did. Those gentlemen Ty sent out here are bent on rescuing you."

Mackenzie was annoyed. "From what?"

"Life." He shrugged. "Yourself? Daisy? I don't know."

"You mean because I'm a single mother."

"Sure. Apparently Ty believes—"

"Ty needs to get bent." Mackenzie forked her cake. "I don't even know what that means, exactly, but I heard someone say it one day and it totally describes what Ty can do to himself."

He laughed. "Good cake."

She watched him happily munching away, not caring at all that his decision to stay had completely upended her world. He had no idea how crazy she was about him—or she'd bet he'd run like the wind. She glared at him. "So you're going to rescue me from the three stooges?"

"No." Justin shook his head. "My role is the innocent bystander."

"So what was Daisy doing in your bed?" She hated to ask but had to know.

"Probably what any red-blooded female would want to do."

She sniffed. "Not any red-blooded female."

"You win. I think she may have had the wrong room."

Mackenzie gave him a cool look. "Daisy never, ever gets the wrong room."

"Really?" He perked up. "Thanks for the ego boost."

Her cool expression went straight to hard stink-eye. "None intended. Just fact."

"Truthfully, it wasn't the most pleasant experience."

"I don't think I believe you," Mackenzie said sweetly.

He put a hand over hers, startling her. "Enough teasing. You know very well I have as much interest in Daisy as I do in wearing wet socks."

His hand was so warm over hers, so strong. She nodded. "I know. I'm sorry. I have no business saying anything—"

"Stop." He squeezed her fingers lightly. "This is your ranch."

"Still, your personal life is your business. If you're really staying, we should establish that up front. You don't worry about my three new hands, and I won't poke my nose into your business."

"Maybe I like your nose—" he lifted her hand to his mouth ever so slowly, kissed it "—in my business."

Her breath caught. His gaze held hers, mesmerizing yet somehow gentle.

She pulled her hand away. "Listen, Justin. You're going—now you're staying. I don't know what to think."

"I understand." He got up and put his dishes in the dishwasher after rinsing them.

Drat. He would be a dish rinser. She silently approved.

"I'm going to hit the hay. By now maybe the fellows are asleep."

She raised a brow. "I can't tell if you like them, or if you view them as carbuncles you have to deal with."

"You don't have the corner on a little healthy jealousy," he said, winking at her before closing the door behind him.

Stunned, she sat glued to her stool for a second, then

shot to the window. Justin walked across to the bunk-house, his big shoulders visible in the darkness.

Unless she was mistaken, that big man had come on to her in a big way. Almost like he'd decided to stay because of her. A feeling of warmth spread over her.

"You like him, don't you?"

Mackenzie squealed and whirled around. "You scared me!"

Suz got back on her stool, her spiky hair awry. "I couldn't sleep. Decided to come get another piece of this cake. Carbs will do something for me, if not make me sleep, then wake me up enough to start filling out some college apps. By the way, I checked on the munchkins. Sleeping like lambs." She cut the cake, glancing up at Mackenzie. "I don't even have to ask if you like Justin. I can tell you do."

Mackenzie returned to her stool. "He's a nice man. Can we talk about college? Where are you planning on applying?"

"Everywhere and anywhere. I'll have to take the MCAT first, the medical school examination." Suz sighed as she ate her cake. "This, I missed."

"I have some money saved—"

"So do I. Thank you, sister dear. But you don't have to take care of me anymore. I'm a big girl, you know." She smiled at her sister. "I love you for it, though. You just don't always have to be mother hen."

"Mom and Dad left us money. They wanted you to have an education," Mackenzie said softly. "You've never touched your part."

"I don't need my part. I don't need much to live on." Suz looked around the kitchen. "If I never spent any of what you call my part, would we have enough to hang on to this place?"

"Suz—"

"Would we?"

Mackenzie looked at her sister. "I know what you're trying to do."

"You *think* you know what I'm trying to do."

"You're trying to figure out how the girls can grow up here and have the same wonderful childhoods we did." Mackenzie looked at her little sister. "We had good childhoods because Mom and Dad worked hard. It wasn't about the ranch so much as it was about our parents. They loved us. They took good care of us."

"It was partially the ranch," Suz said stubbornly. "And you're not respecting the Hanging H when you talk that way. Mom and Dad built this up from nothing. It's the heart and soul of who we are."

Suz gazed at her, unblinking. She never wore makeup. There were tats and piercings and hair dye but never makeup. And somehow her eyes were still so very expressive.

"I know you're right," Mackenzie said, "and I love that you're trying to honor our parents' memory. But I think they'd want you to have your money for a rainy day. So you don't have to take loans for college or medical school. For whatever you may need. Remember how hard Mom and Dad worked to build the Hanging H? They wouldn't want you to struggle as hard as they did."

"Do I get any say in this? A vote?"

"Of course you do."

"Good. Because it didn't feel like it there for a minute." Suz ate some cake, waved her fork. "I've lived in Africa for a year. I just don't have needs like other people do. It's hard to think about material things when I understand what people live without. And what I developed a great appreciation for was home."

Mackenzie sighed. "I haven't even had a chance to see your Africa photos yet. Let's leave this for another day."

"It's not a decision that's going to wait long. You've got four hands signed on. And Jade told me that you were planning on selling out by Christmas."

"I was going to tell you—"

"I know. You were going to tell me when you quit mooning after the cowboy."

"I really was going to discuss it with you. I wouldn't make the decision without you. But I didn't know if you planned on coming home, Suz. Truthfully, I had no way of knowing if you would stay with the Peace Corps. Your letters sounded like you were so happy."

Suz waved a hand again. "This is why Daisy's buzzing around here, trying to steal your man. She knows you're weakening."

"I am not weakening!"

"It's clear I came home in the nick of time." Suz carried her plate to the dishwasher, then, without rinsing, just placed it inside. She turned to grin at Mackenzie. "I know. Your pet peeve." She pulled the plate back out and gave it a swift rinse before replacing it. "I don't want to sell the family home or the ranch. None of it. I'd rather see you married to one of the three new guys than—"

"Married!" Mackenzie shook her head. "You can forget that nonsense right now. I'm never going through that again."

"Speak in haste—"

"It's not haste. Marriage isn't for me." Not even to the hunky man who'd just kissed her hand. Luckily he was a rebel who had no interest in settling down.

"One of us is going to have to run Daisy off for good," Suz said darkly. "Remember when our folks passed, she was like a vampire, hanging around looking to suck the dollar bills out of this place."

"There are no dollar bills to suck. If we keep the ranch, we're going to have to think of a way to make it profitable. It's big enough that we could take in boarders," she said, looking around the kitchen.

"No!"

Mackenzie blinked. "All right. No boarders."

"It wouldn't be right. We have the babies to think of. I don't want anybody around them that we don't know."

"All right. Any other ideas?"

"I'll work for a couple of years, then apply to medical school."

"No!" Mackenzie said, protesting as forcefully as her sister had about boarders. "*That* is not an option."

"We'll think of something." Suz drummed her fingers. "I can be very creative."

"That worries me." Mackenzie could hear the wheels turning in her sister's head.

"Whatever we do, it has to be something that keeps Daisy from catwalking around here all the time, annoying the crap out of me."

"She really bugs you, doesn't she?"

"Yes." Suz got up to look out the kitchen window. "She's after Justin."

Mackenzie shook her head. "It's doesn't matter."

"It does. I can't bear to let her win." Suz giggled. "At anything. In fact, I like to see her lose."

"Suz!"

"She deserves it." Her sister laughed again. "You're too tenderhearted. Be tenderhearted about our home, okay?" She kissed Mackenzie on the cheek and opened the kitchen door.

"Where are you going?"

"To see the three musketeers. They might be up playing cards or something. They look like the types that would have something going on in the wee hours. 'Night, sis."

Suz drifted out the door. Mackenzie watched her from the kitchen window. Sure enough, the bunkhouse door opened and shut with alacrity, and more lights went on inside.

The new guys had no idea what they were in for.

Mackenzie turned out the kitchen lights and went to check on her babies. Like Suz had said, they were sleeping like lambs. She loved her daughters so much. It felt as if her heart was tied to them in some way she couldn't have explained to anyone.

Maybe Suz was right. The Hanging H would be a wonderful place for the girls to grow up. Deep in her heart, she'd like them to have what she and her sister had as kids. Yet it cost money—a lot of money—to pay the bills at a ranch that wasn't bringing in income. She'd been dipping into her own inheritance to cover expenses.

The nursery smelled like baby powder and freshly laundered linen. She sat down in a rocker for a moment, enjoying the gentleness and peace in the room. In the soft glow from the night-light, Mackenzie thought life could probably never get better than this.

She thought about Justin kissing her and about Daisy leaving his bedroom. He just didn't strike her as a dishonest man. And Daisy could be such a finagler. Suz was right: Daisy had long had her eyes on the Hanging H acreage. Set on prime real estate, near to usable roads but back far enough from town to feel private, the ranch had intrinsic value for those who might dream of large homes designed in the new architecture. Not like their traditional home now, with its quaint rooms and hidden staircase and wide window views.

This was home, full of happy memories and the misty patina of childhood dreams. The four men she'd hired would help her get the place back in shape to put on the market—there was no other way she could see to secure the future for her daughters, for Suz and even for Bridesmaids Creek. Maybe someone with money would buy the place, bring it back to its former glory, where it could once again give back to the community she loved so much.

As for Justin, she was just too close to the past to count on a man Ty had brought here for the specific purpose of rescuing her. Ty thought she needed that, but she'd do just fine on her own.

"IT'S NOT GOING to work, fellows." Suz stared at the four men lounging around the room, settled in leather recliners and on the huge circular sectional that, despite its age, still looked in good condition. Someone had been smoking a cigar, but Suz supposed it was likely that worse had been smoked under this roof.

With the three new guys, anything could happen. They had a bit of a wild look to them, not too long out of the heat of a war zone. Justin was his cool-cucumber self. Suz eyed him, and he eyed her in return. She didn't know the man well enough to say, but she had the feeling that cowboy wasn't a smoker. "I get the plan. I even appreciate that you've taken the time to dream something up to try to help my sister."

This she directed at Squint, Frog and Sam, as she was pretty certain Justin hadn't had any part in the idea they'd sprung on her. "My sister isn't going to get married to one of you in order to have a father for her children. She has one of those, and he's a louse, and I can tell you that even though you're offering to sign away any financial or gainful rights to the ranch, Mackenzie will never stand at an altar again. At least not in the near future, and I believe she's putting the ranch on the market as soon as you get the place fixed up. She mentioned something about wanting to be out of here by Christmas."

Sam glanced at Justin. "Do you have anything to say, or are you just going to sit there like a bump on a log?"

Justin looked at his newfound companions but didn't say a word. Suz supposed the question didn't merit an answer, and, anyway, Justin wasn't the type of man who would be pushed into any harebrained schemes.

Marrying her sister off was certainly the most foolish scheme that had been floated. "Got any more practical ideas under those Stetsons?"

Justin laughed, which she thought might be rude. Was he even trying to help her sister? At least the new guys were focused on the problem, which was dire.

"Dig out your folks' business model and records from the days of the haunted house," Justin said, stunning her.

"Well, Mr. Helpful, that's not going to work, either. My sister thinks we're moving. Not opening a business."

"Tell her it's just for this last season. Sort of a goodbye to Bridesmaids Creek." Justin's gaze gleamed, his eyes intent, and she realized he'd been working on the problem all along, just waiting for the right time to spring it.

She frowned. "With you four as ringleaders?"

"Well, we all need jobs," Frog pointed out. "And we'd like to stay here."

"I don't get what's in it for you," Suz said.

"Money," Squint said. "And this place is nice. It's kind of storybook."

"And you have your eyes on Daisy Donovan." Suz noticed none of the three new guys seemed bothered by that pronouncement, but then Frog spoke up.

"Not me. Not my type," he said, his tone certain. "I go for the real wild girls."

Wilder than Daisy? Suz wrinkled her nose, suddenly aware that Frog was looking at *her*. Intently. Like he had something on his mind.

He wasn't suggesting that she was wild? What would make him think that? "Er—"

"Look, Daisy's a nice woman, I'm sure," Justin said, "but you fellows best cast your nets elsewhere."

"Why?" Frog demanded, his face a bit crestfallen. "We're not horning in on you. You've got a thing for the boss lady, anyone with one eye can see that—"

Frog fell silent, dead silent, at Justin's raised brow. Suz stared at the big man, ready to hear the truth. "Well, Cowboy? Do you have a thing for my sister?"

Chapter Nine

Justin found himself in the hot seat unexpectedly, and he knew it was best to get off in a hurry. "Don't listen to our friends. I've learned they talk a lot but say little of importance."

"Maybe we talk a lot but say a lot of importance that you don't want to admit," Frog said.

Suz was staring at him. "You're not denying it, Justin."

"I don't have to." He met the eyes of each of his new friends, daring them to say another thing. They all looked away from him after a moment—except Suz.

"O-*kay*," Suz said. "Anyway, what we need to do is figure out how to get my sister out of her pickle. Get *us* out of our pickle," she amended. "Any and all good ideas will be considered. For the sake of my nieces."

A sideways sensation hit Justin at the mention of those four tiny dolls. They deserved more than they were going to get out of life. He didn't need little sister to spell it out for him. Deadbeat Dad was long gone, and Mackenzie and her babies would be living off their wits. Suz was a different animal altogether, obviously a tough survivor. So was Mackenzie, but she had a soft edge to her. Soft, sexy, rounded edges.

"Aw, he's not going to step up to the plate," Frog said,

staring at Justin derisively. "So here's my good idea. Marry me, Suz."

Suz blinked. Justin stayed out of this new twist. If Frog wanted to get tossed back into the pond on his head by Suz, that was no concern of his.

"Marry you?" Suz scoffed. "I said come up with a *good* idea."

Justin laughed. "She has you there."

Suz got up. "Marriage isn't the answer for anyone."

Justin crossed his legs. "You're too young to be so cynical."

"Not cynical. Practical," Suz replied.

He thought she was adorable in a little sister sort of way. "I agree marriage is a bad idea."

"Yeah," she said, looking at Frog. "Any woman who would marry a man named Frog needs to have her head examined."

Justin took pity on his new buddy. "Take it easy on the man. He's just trying to help."

"Yeah," Sam said. "Does anybody think that little Jade mama might be open to a date?"

Justin shook his head. "You have to ask to find out."

"Anyway," Squint said, "you're all too chicken. Let's head into town. Hunt up some trouble."

"We're trying to solve the Hanging H problem," Justin reminded the room at large.

"Yeah, but I want to find that ornery little brunette with the loud bike," Squint said. "I like my ladies loud and wild."

"If you go for Crazy Daisy," Suz said, "you deserve everything you get."

"Looking forward to that." Squint winked at them and went out the door. Sam looked disgusted, Frog surprised.

Justin shook his head. "Let's table this meeting. We'll meet again when somebody has a real idea."

"I really think," Frog said, staring at Suz like he wanted to melt into her arms, "that you should let me take you into town for an ice-cream cone, Miss Suz."

"I've got ice cream in the freezer. Sorry, Frog." She drifted out the door, and Justin looked at his buddy with pity.

"Don't be discouraged. She's got a lot on her mind," Justin said.

"Pretty sure she shot me down," Frog said, his shoulders drooping.

"It'll work out, maybe," Justin said. "Good night, gentlemen." He headed off to his room, needing to disconnect from all the angst being shared. How to save the Hanging H—if Mackenzie even wanted it saved. He thought again about the murder near the Hanging H that had ruined the haunted house, wondered if that was the reason Mackenzie didn't want to open it again.

Maybe worrying about Mackenzie was a waste of time. Could be she didn't want him thinking about her situation. Maybe she'd shoot him down as hard as Suz had shot down Frog. Those Hawthorne girls seemed pretty independent. Wild child Suz with a guy named Frog? Not a chance.

For starters, Frog had to reveal his real name if he was going to get the girl. But Justin figured advice to the lovelorn should stay in Madame Matchmaker's capable hands, because he had no desire to get involved in small-town love affairs and soap operas.

Me? I'm going to have to get the girl the old-fashioned way.

I'm going to win her.

Mackenzie wasn't looking for another man, as Suz had

pointed out. In fact, it might be easier to be Frog with his insane crush on Suz.

He'd never let long odds stop him before.

"You've got the whole thing wrong," Mackenzie told Ty a week later when she ran into him at The Wedding Diner. "You sent four bachelors to my place on purpose."

Ty looked amused. "Would you rather I sent four happily married men?"

Mackenzie glanced around the diner, remembering her father bringing her there to have lunch and a piece of cake. They'd had those father–daughter luncheons many times over the years, as he'd also done with Suz, calling them his special times with his children. Maybe he'd done it to give her mother a break from the kids, she thought fondly. She would have understood that—right now Betty and Jade were watching the quadruplets. As much as she loved her children, a mini-break was nice, too. "You won't believe this, but the last thing I want in my life is a man. I just don't have room for one."

He winked. "There is always room for the right man."

"But I didn't elect you my matchmaker," Mackenzie protested, knowing by the gleam in his eye that her friend wasn't listening to her with any remorse. "When I want a matchmaker, I'll go to Madame Matchmaker."

"I'm not stealing any business from her." Ty grinned. "As far as I'm concerned, I owe you one from the first time."

"No one could have foretold how Tommy would feel about becoming a father to four children."

Ty's expression turned dark. "Look, Mackenzie, not to rub salt in the wound, but Tommy Fields never deserved you. He'd always considered himself a hot item with the ladies. I just believed him when he said he'd changed."

She shrugged. "I don't care anymore."

"I guess you do a little," he said softly, "or you wouldn't be so annoyed about the perfectly macho specimens I put out at your ranch."

She made a face. "So you admit you were being a Nosy Ned when you put that package together and sent it my way."

"They needed a job. You deserve better choices for a father for your daughters. How am I a bad guy?" He winked at her. "Look, you're young, Mackenzie."

"Thirty."

"Young. You're beautiful, smart and talented. You deserve a great guy."

She sniffed. "Why not you?" she demanded, just to wind him up. Ty would never settle down, never.

He looked aggrieved and reached to hold her hand in his. "Your hand is warm from your coffee cup."

She raised a brow.

"Friends don't let friends marry inappropriately. And I'm so inappropriate."

She laughed. "Yes, you are."

"I would marry you, you know, if I hadn't sent you better options," he said, his tone convincing and yet the expression on his face somehow not.

"You're such a fibber. You'll never get married."

"Nope," he said happily, releasing her hand. "But I'd call it a day and go home happy if you'd get married again."

"You realize one of those men has a thing for Daisy—"

"That's a misfire," he said, frowning. "Squint needs to have his head examined. Think he left a critical part of his brain back in Afghanistan."

"And one might be developing a thing for Suz."

He pondered that news. "Not exactly a misfire, but not exactly encouraging, either."

"That's my sister," Mackenzie said. "Speak with respect."

"I'm just saying she's young—she's not pliable."

Mackenzie laughed. "You mean she wouldn't allow you to manipulate her. I'm completely on to you."

Justin walked into the diner. Everybody turned to look at him, and Mackenzie could easily see why he'd draw attention. He was so big and tall and he carried himself well, his aura strong and commanding. Her heart jumped a little.

If she was going to think about dating again, Justin would definitely be high on her list.

He'd be the only man she'd want on her list.

"Hi," Justin said, sliding into the booth next to her. "Who are we gossiping about today?"

He was muscular and warm beside her. Mackenzie told herself to ignore the sudden hormone surge. "I believe Ty was talking about you."

Justin eyed Ty. "Matchmaking again?"

Ty laughed. "You know me too well."

"Does Madame Matchmaker know you're horning in on her area of expertise?"

"She gave me her blessings." Ty winked at Mackenzie. "I have to go. Tell your sister no go on the new guys. Those are all for you."

Ty sauntered off, paid his tab and kissed Jane Chatham goodbye. Mackenzie wrinkled her nose. "He thinks so much of himself." She noticed Justin wasn't in a big hurry to shift to the other side of the booth.

After a moment he seemed to remember where he was and moved to the other side. She kind of wished he hadn't.

"Let me ask you something," Justin said. "Is there any

circumstance under which you'd rethink bringing back your family's business?"

His question stunned her. "I haven't thought about it. All my time and energy is devoted to my daughters. In fact, I need to be getting back. It's about time for their lunch."

He caught her hand. "Give me five minutes. Then I'll head back and give you a hand."

"I didn't hire you to be a—"

"Hanny."

She sighed, put her shoulder bag back down in the seat. "That's such a stupid expression. Only Ty could have thought of it."

"I like the little ladies." He looked at her. "I have the strangest sensation you don't really want to move."

"Nobody ever wants to move. Sometimes you suck it up and know that life will be good anyway."

"Yeah." He rubbed her fingers, and tiny sparks tingled inside her. She realized the diner had gone totally silent, everyone focused on them.

Oh, boy. She discreetly pulled her fingers away, then hid them in her lap.

"Sorry," he said, glancing around. "I forgot we're in BC."

For a moment, she had, too. It had felt like they were in their own world.

Which was probably not a good thing.

The people in the diner—folks she'd known all her life—slowly turned back to their meals, but the buzz around them was low and excited. Definitely the gossip bandwagon was rolling merrily along now. "To answer your question honestly and fairly, I wish I could keep the ranch for the girls. But it's precisely because of the girls that I won't."

"I get it. I really do. I grew up in Whitefish, Montana. I'll never live there." He shrugged. "Life moves on."

"It's not just that," Mackenzie began, and the diner door opened again and Daisy walked in with Frog on her arm looking like the cat that ate the canary.

"That's not right," Mackenzie said, and Justin turned to see what was going on.

"No, it's not," he said.

Daisy and Frog slid into the booth.

"Hello, boss lady," Frog said. "Justin, thanks for the afternoon off. I'm putting it to good advantage." He beamed at Daisy, who gave him such a sexy look that Mackenzie thought the napkins at the table might combust.

But then Daisy's gaze slid to Justin, and Mackenzie knew it was all a show.

Jane Chatham came over. "What can I get everyone?"

"Spice cake and an iced tea for me," Daisy said. "I want a piece with as much frosting as you can manage, Jane."

Frog looked besotted. "I'll have the same. Not so much frosting, though."

"I'll just stick with iced tea," Mackenzie said, wishing she could take off. She would go, except that Justin was looking at her with such an intense stare that her heart pounded. She wasn't about to leave him to Daisy's wiles.

That was a terrible thought she shouldn't even be thinking.

Didn't matter. "And a piece of spice cake," she added. *Might as well go the whole mile.*

"I figured you'd be watching your weight, Micki," Daisy said, bringing up an old nickname Mackenzie had always despised.

"I'll have some pecan pie," Justin said, cutting through the sudden tension at the table. "Hot coffee with that, if you don't mind, Jane."

"You should let me tell your fortune, Justin," Jane said, and Mackenzie looked at Justin to gauge his reaction.

Which was slightly amused.

"If it comes with the pie, I might take you up on it," Justin said, his tone easy.

It hit Mackenzie that Justin was trying to fit into the ways of BC, which probably weren't like any other town he'd lived in. Mackenzie hid a smile.

"Do let her, Justin," Daisy said. "You'll be surprised what Jane can tell you."

"I don't really believe in fortune-telling and horoscopes and hocus-pocus. No offense, Jane," Justin said.

Jane smiled. "None taken. How's the family in Whitefish?"

He blinked. "They're fine, thank you."

"Knee hasn't been bothering you as much, has it?"

"No, ma'am, it hasn't."

Daisy giggled. Frog looked at her as if a goddess had landed in his sphere and he couldn't quite figure out how it had happened.

"Four drinks and desserts coming right up." Jane went off, her stride all-business, as it always was. Mackenzie looked at Justin.

"She doesn't really tell fortunes as much as she reads people," Mackenzie told him.

"She listens to gossip very well," Justin said. "But what the heck. I'll play."

"Gossip?" Daisy looked adorably confused; clearly she'd decided adorable was the key to Justin's heart. "What does gossip have to do with anything?"

"I told her husband down at the feed store today that my father was having a bit of trouble on the ranch in Whitefish," Justin said. His gaze hooked on Mackenzie's. "I also mentioned that my knee was doing a lot better."

Mackenzie shook her head. "When is Ty leaving, anyway?"

"You're not going with him, are you?" Daisy asked, her tone sweetly horrified. Designed to suck up to Justin's ego.

"Staying right here." He leaned back in the booth, winking at Mackenzie. "Not going any place anytime soon."

Warmth ran all over Mackenzie. She didn't look away from Justin's gaze, even though it was hot, hot, hot. No, she didn't look away, even though Daisy and Frog were kind of gawking at the two of them. Jane dropped off their desserts and drinks, just as they'd ordered, which seemed to surprise everyone at the table.

Then Justin shocked the entire diner by reaching over and placing his cowboy hat on top of Mackenzie's head.

"Little mama," he said, "you're the sexiest thing I've ever laid eyes on, and that's a fact."

And that was the moment Mackenzie felt herself falling.

It felt unexpectedly wonderful.

"No, Frog," Daisy said, glaring past him. He'd tried to plant a kiss on her and she was having none of that, as Justin could have foretold. In the shadows cast by the declining sun just dissipating around the barn, Justin shook his head. In a minute, he'd save Frog from himself—but not quite yet. It wouldn't hurt him to figure out that he wasn't quite the gift Daisy had led him to think he was. Oh, there'd be a little bit of ego bruising, but it wouldn't last long. Frog would snap back.

Frog tried again, a bit oblivious to the fact that he was out of Daisy's league. He'd really bought into Daisy's flirtation, which was dumb. Daisy flirted with every man.

Justin walked from the barn to the house on his way

inside to find Mackenzie and the babies. "Frog, I need you to change out every single lightbulb in the spotlights and the lanterns on the corrals."

His demand seemed to jerk Frog out of his Daisy spell. "All right. Night, Daisy."

"Good night," Daisy said absently.

Frog ambled off, his shoulders slumping a bit. Mackenzie came outside, looking from Justin to Daisy. "What are you doing here, Daisy?"

"I heard a piece of gossip in town that you might be reopening the Haunted H, Mackenzie," Daisy said. "I was a little surprised when Jane Chatham told me, because I know how devastated you were when that man died out here. They never figured out what happened to him, did they?"

Mackenzie's face turned pale as the moon. Daisy looked pleased with herself.

"That was ten years ago, Daisy." She turned to Justin. "I got your text. You're welcome to dinner if you'd like." She closed the door, leaving Justin with Daisy outside.

"What was that all about?" Justin asked Daisy, knowing full well she had something up her tight sleeve.

"Well, if Mackenzie hadn't slammed the door in my face, I was going to tell her I'd be happy to help with the Haunted H. I'm good with kids," Daisy said, turning on the cute as hard as she could.

Daisy help Mackenzie? He doubted that. "I'm sure she got the message. Good night."

He went inside. Mackenzie sat at the kitchen table with the four babies in their carriers, gently wiping their faces. She didn't look at him.

"So," he said, going to pick up Haven—she'd already

been given the cleaning treatment, so she smelled like sweet lavender. "You going to tell me what happened out here? Or are you going to let Daisy keep digging at you?"

Chapter Ten

Mackenzie didn't say anything, and Justin thought he heard a sniffle, like maybe she was trying to hold back tears. He didn't know her well enough to say definitely, but Mackenzie didn't strike him as much of a crier.

Suz wandered into the room. "Here, give me Thing One," she said, trying to take Haven from him.

"Get your own Thing," he said, holding the baby against his chest so Suz couldn't get her.

Shrugging, Suz took Thing Number Two—Holly— out of her basket, kissed her and then caught a glimpse of Mackenzie's face. "Hey! Is he making you cry?" She glared at Justin. "You put Thing One back in her carrier and get out!"

"No!" Mackenzie shook her head. "I'm not crying, and nobody's putting any Things back!" She laughed, wiping her nose on a baby washcloth. "I wish you hadn't started calling the girls Things. It makes conversation really interesting."

"Yeah, well. I've been reading Dr. Seuss to the girls as part of their early reading program." She glared again at Justin. "You'd best watch yourself, Cowboy."

"Suz." Mackenzie took Heather out of her carrier and sat down to feed her. Justin couldn't bear it because that meant Hope was left with nobody to hold her, so he picked her up in his other arm. "Justin didn't do anything. I just let stupid old Daisy drag up ancient history. I shouldn't, but it happened."

"Is she still here? Because if she is, I'm going to kick her ass." Suz went to the window, but Justin had heard Daisy's motorcycle roar off a few minutes ago, saving her from the ass-kicking he had no doubt Suz could dish out. "Anyway, what's she hanging around here for?"

"She had a little outing with Frog." Mackenzie's gaze met Justin's. He got that jolt he always felt around Mackenzie and wished she'd let down her guard just an inch. An inch was all he'd need to get inside her heart.

"Daisy and Frog?" Suz came back to join them. Justin thought it was interesting that Suz looked surprised, and maybe not pleasantly. "Why would he want to take out the wicked witch of Bridesmaids Creek? Quite stupid, if you ask me. But that's a man for you." She drifted out of the room with Holly, cooing softly to her.

Mackenzie kissed the top of Heather's head. "Why was Frog hanging around with Daisy?"

"Because your sister turned him down flat as a very old pancake." Justin sighed, but the feeling of the two babies in his arms was at least comforting. "He had a momentary brain fart is the best way I can explain it."

"Frog seems to suffer from that."

"Yes, but don't tell Suz. Injured pride has been known to send a man into other arms."

Mackenzie didn't look convinced. "Weak argument."

"I'm just saying I think Daisy has strong allure. Frog's pride was dented. He folded when Daisy asked him to go running around today. But I suspect he'd rather Suz look on him with some fondness."

Mackenzie didn't say anything to that. She carried Heather from the room, and he followed. Together they placed the babies on a soft pallet in front of the fireplace, joining their sister Holly.

"You ever going to tell me about this information Daisy threw out that upset you so much?"

He sat on the sofa; she sat on the floor with her babies. He wished he dared pull out his phone and snap a photo of her. There was just nothing more beautiful than Mackenzie and those babies, a perfect four of a kind. A man could get real used to being around this little family.

"I don't like to talk about it. Suffice it to say someone died here. It made everything ugly. Before that happened, everyone looked at our children's haunted house as a wonderful, safe event. When the murderer was never found, it really hurt business. Mom and Dad held off as long as they could, and the town tried really hard to help. But the next year, attendance really dropped." She took a deep breath. "It's hard to erase such a stain, and my parents' health went down fast after that. First Dad went, and then Mom about five months later." She looked at Justin. "So, no, I'll never, ever reopen the haunted house."

"I don't blame you." He could make a little more sense of Ty's eagerness to help Mackenzie—although he was just as certain that Ty's idea of finding her a husband wasn't as brilliant as Ty thought it was. What he wanted to do more than anything was hold her in his arms, protect her from the sad memories he knew she could never forget. "How can I help you?"

"You can't." She looked at him. "But it means a lot that you want to, and I thank you for that."

He wanted to help her. Justin had never felt helpless before, but the fact was, he had nothing to offer Mackenzie. He could work at the ranch as long as she needed him, but so could the new guys. They were good men, hard workers. Eventually Mackenzie would sell the place—she'd said by Christmas.

There wasn't anything he could do for her.

She shocked him when she got up off the floor and sat next to him on the sofa, gazing into his eyes. "You don't have to rescue me. You don't have to take care of me. I know Ty sent you here on a mercy mission and I appreciate everything you've done. But I promise you, we'll be fine."

We'll be fine. Her and Suz and the angels. He glanced at the four babies on the floor, secure in their soft blankets, in the process of either practicing opening their eyelids or dozing off.

"I know you will." It was true. He wanted to kiss her in the worst way, feel her lips underneath his. Wanted to hold her in his arms. Didn't dare. Making more moves on the boss lady was no way to make her feel good about him staying around. And there was no way he wanted to leave. Mackenzie and her small, seemingly defenseless family had thoroughly stolen his heart.

A tap on the back door caught their attention, and Mackenzie went into the kitchen. Justin stared at the babies, thinking that whatever the ex hadn't seen in being a father to four daughters was completely obvious to him.

Frog, Sam and Squint walked in, following Mackenzie like puppies. "What's going on, fellows?" Justin asked.

"I—we have an idea," Sam said, and Justin thought, *Oh, no.*

"What's going on?" Suz asked, wandering in. "Sounds like Grand Central Station in here. I just started watching *Pride and Prejudice*, the 1940 version, and I can hear you over the Bennet sisters. Which is no easy feat."

She sat down cross-legged next to the blanket and picked up Holly, shooting an annoyed look Frog's way. Justin wondered if she even knew she'd done it.

"Sam has an idea," Justin said, his tone ironic. He arched a brow at Sam. "Go ahead. Share."

Mackenzie waved the men to some flowery chairs near the sofa, and they gawked at the babies.

"Four," Frog said. "I would never have believed all those babies could come out of such a little lady."

"Nice," Squint said. "Graceful even, Frog."

"Sorry." He honestly looked like he might be blushing. "I'm not always gifted with speech."

"No fooling." Suz looked pleased to get a dig in. Justin wondered if she felt more for Frog than she was letting on.

"What's your real name?" Justin demanded. "I can't go on calling you Frog. It's just all wrong," he said to the dark-haired big man.

Frog looked uncomfortable now that all the attention was squarely on him. "Francisco Rodriguez Olivier Grant. Mom was French, Dad was Spanish. They had some debate about how many relations in the family needed to be honored when I was born. Therefore, Frog. Deal with it."

Justin stared at him. "You're definitely not a Francisco."

His buddies laughed. "He's an F-R-O-G," Squint said.

"I think it's lovely," Mackenzie said quickly, and Justin gave her an appreciative look. He found himself feeling a little sorry for the big man.

"It's just a name," Suz said, and Frog perked up a bit. "They're all good names, too."

"My high school and college friends called me Rodriguez," Frog said. "It wasn't until the military that I became Frog."

Suz smiled at him. Practically batted her eyes.

"Now that we have that solved," Mackenzie said with a glance at Justin, "what idea do you want to share, Sam?"

He took a deep breath. "A cattle base, for one thing. You have enough land here to run about two dozen head.

Could do milk goats, too. The whole organic thing has really taken off, and you have a great place here for opening your own organic kitchen and label."

Justin was stunned. "I didn't know you had it in you, Sam. I've misjudged you."

"Easy to do because I'm so quiet," he said, and they all hooted at him.

"Part two of the plan," Squint said, "is to consider storytelling tours. Like survival tours. People are interested in learning how to make their own cheese and raise their own organic food."

"And we'll all dress in costumes," Suz said. "I see where you're going with this."

They all looked at Mackenzie for her reaction. "I don't know what to say," she said, and Justin could tell she was truly caught off guard. "It's actually a brilliant idea."

"It's in the early phase," Frog said. "We've been brainstorming. Once we develop a business plan, we'll bring it to you."

Suz went into the kitchen, then brought back a tray of cookies and a pitcher of milk. "All that brainstorming probably has you hungry," she said, setting the tray down on the coffee table.

Justin noticed she handed Frog a napkin, then flounced over to pick up Heather, who was starting to stir, as if she hadn't treated Frog just a little bit differently than the other men.

"I don't know what to think." Mackenzie went into the kitchen to get a bottle, brought it back and handed it to Suz. "Someone's tummy tanked out a little sooner than her sisters'."

"I know how she feels," Frog said earnestly. "I'm always hungry."

Justin looked at Mackenzie. "Any chance you could

hang on to this place if a workable business model was drawn up? You're busy with the babies, but these three seem pretty eager to keep their bunks here."

"Yes, we are," Squint said. "I never imagined I'd like living in a small town, but I have to say after Afghanistan I have a whole new perspective on small-town friendly."

Justin leaned back in his chair, pondering Squint's words. He had to give the three amigos points for coming up with an idea—and maybe not even a half-bad idea—for trying to help Mackenzie and Suz out. He studied the sisters—polar opposites—and wondered how Mackenzie would feel if she knew he felt the same as the three amigos.

As if this had become sort of a home—and she was the person he wanted to come home to every night, forever.

Not long after the guys had shared their business idea, they left, and to Mackenzie's surprise her sister went with them. "You don't mind?" Suz had asked Mackenzie, and Justin said he'd stay and help put the babies to bed, so Suz had bolted out the door.

They were going into town to "hunt up trouble," as Sam said, and Suz had said trouble sounded good to her. Mackenzie wondered if Justin would have liked to go hunting trouble, too.

"You could have gone with them." Mackenzie closed the nursery door after making sure the baby monitor was on and the babies were totally settled.

Justin gave her a long look she couldn't quite read. "I could have. Didn't want to get in the way of Frog trying to figure out Suz."

She smiled as they walked back into the family room. "You really think she'll look at him twice after he was seen out with Daisy?"

"That did seem to tweak your sister a bit." He sat on the sofa, lounging, long and lean and sexy. "In fact, I'd bet that's why she so eagerly went with them tonight."

Mackenzie looked at the tray of cookies that had been polished off pretty well. "I'm going to get a cup of hot tea. Can I get you one?"

He followed her into the kitchen. "I'll take a glass of iced tea." He then proceeded to get it himself. Justin put the teakettle on to heat while she got down a teacup and saucer.

It struck her that she liked this, the sort of family feeling of togetherness that she felt with Justin.

"So what did you really think about the boys' idea?" he asked.

She put some loose-leaf tea into a tea ball and set it into her cup. "I'm going to think it over."

He turned her toward him. "I know you'd like to stay here, Mackenzie. When I look at this house, I think of you. It's like you're a part of it."

"Thank you." His hand lingered at her elbow for just a moment, a moment too short.

"Don't let Daisy drive you away," he said.

She hesitated. "Daisy has nothing to do with it."

"Felt like she struck a nerve today with that speech about the dead guy."

A chill ran over Mackenzie. "I don't like it, but it doesn't define whether I sell or not. It's just about finances."

"And leaving memories behind."

She studied him as he leaned against the counter, his boots crossed, his gaze on her. "Maybe. Sometimes."

He nodded. "I understand wanting a fresh start."

The kettle whistled and he reached behind her to turn it off, brushing her arm ever so slightly. He looked down at her and then lowered his mouth to hers.

FREE Merchandise is 'in the Cards' for you!

Dear Reader,

We're giving away FREE MERCHANDISE!

Seriously, we'd like to reward you for reading this novel by giving you **FREE MERCHANDISE** worth over $20. And no purchase is necessary!

You see the Jack of Hearts sticker above? Paste that sticker in the box on the Free Merchandise Voucher inside. Return the Voucher promptly…and we'll send you valuable Free Merchandise!

Thanks again for reading one of our novels—and enjoy your Free Merchandise with our compliments!

Pam Powers

Pam Powers

P.S. Look inside to see what Free Merchandise is **"in the cards"** for you!

W

e'd like to send you two free books like the one you are enjoying now. Your two books have a combined price of over $10, but they are yours to keep absolutely FREE! We'll even send you 2 wonderful surprise gifts. You can't lose!

REMEMBER: Your Free Merchandise, consisting of **2 Free Books** and **2 Free Gifts**, is worth over $20.00! No purchase is necessary, so please send for your Free Merchandise today.

Get TWO FREE GIFTS!

We'll also send you two wonderful FREE GIFTS (worth about $10), in addition to your 2 Free books!

Visit us at:

www.ReaderService.com

FREE MERCHANDISE VOUCHER

2 FREE BOOKS and 2 FREE GIFTS

Please send my Free Merchandise, consisting of **2 Free Books** and **2 Free Mystery Gifts**. I understand that I am under no obligation to buy anything, as explained on the back of this card.

154/354 HDL GEYY

Please Print

FIRST NAME

LAST NAME

ADDRESS

APT.#   CITY

STATE/PROV.   ZIP/POSTAL CODE

NO PURCHASE NECESSARY!

AR-714-FM13

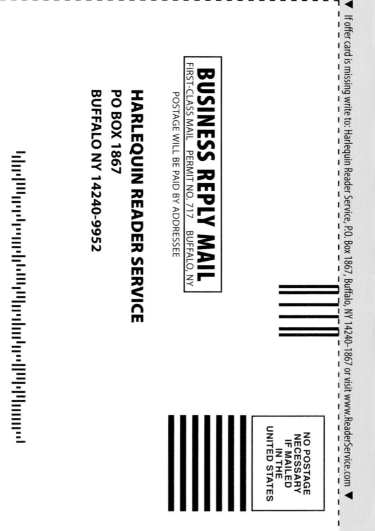

Thankfully. Mackenzie didn't think she could have waited any longer to kiss Justin. He kissed her so sweetly, then turned more demanding as she melted into him. She heard a little moan, realized it was coming from her. Ran her hands around his back to hold him close—sank into his body as he devoured her mouth.

She'd never been kissed like this. *Don't stop—this time, don't stop.* She felt as though she was going to jump out of her skin if she didn't get closer to him.

Bed, she wanted to say, but her mouth wouldn't say the word. "Make love to me," she whispered, her mouth desperately getting out what she felt, and he scooped her into his arms to carry her down the hall.

He glanced at the old-fashioned four-poster bed dressed in sky blue and white. "Feminine. Just like you."

He placed her on the bed, making short work of her clothes. She just as quickly got rid of his, dying to get her hands on the muscles and tanned skin she'd watched working many times. His hands were work-rough but gentle on her, and she moaned again, pulling him into the bed with her. He stroked a strand of her hair from her face.

"You're beautiful," he told her, then kissed her, taking his time. Mackenzie closed her eyes, letting his lips work magic on her.

More magic as he held her in his arms and made long, gentle love to her. Mackenzie felt herself waking, coming to life, amazed by how much wonder a man could make her feel. Like a princess, kissed awake by a prince, Mackenzie wanted the magic to last forever.

JUSTIN JERKED AWAKE at the sound of motorcycles roaring up the drive. Sudden baby tears and snuffles jerked him out of bed. He glanced at his watch—two o'clock in the morning. There shouldn't be motorcycles gunning out-side at this hour.

"What's going on?" Mackenzie asked, sitting up, switching on a bedside lamp. "Oh, the babies are awake. They don't usually get up this soon. All that noise must have woken them." She jumped out of bed and pulled on a robe, giving Justin a brief glimpse of bare skin he wished he could drag back to bed to kiss for a few more hours.

"I'll check out what's going on," he said. "You get the girls calmed down and I'll come help you."

"Thank you."

She dashed from the room. He'd sensed her hesitation, like she didn't want to accept that she needed his help.

He went to the kitchen door and hauled it open, pre-pared to give someone heck for being rodeo-loud when there were babies asleep—everyone in BC would know that it needed to be walking-on-eggshells quiet around here at this hour.

About six motorcycles wheeled around at the top of the drive—damn it, six—then drove past him, heading down the road, gunning like mad. One did a wheelie as it went by, and he recognized Daisy's long bronze hair and tight black gear.

He waited, but they didn't return. Damn them, they'd done a drive-by on purpose, either to wake the babies or to haze Mackenzie.

He went back inside, locking the door behind him. He headed straight to the nursery. Mackenzie had four unhappy little girls on her hands, and he couldn't blame them.

"Come here," he told Hope, picking her up. "Bottles or breast at this hour?"

"Bottles, I think. They're too upset from the noise." She rocked Haven, feeding her. "What was that?"

He turned on some soothing music on his phone, Brahms's lullaby, as he popped a bottle into Hope's mouth, soothing the two remaining girls so they could relax long enough to wait their turns. "About six motorcycles."

"Daisy's gang."

"Gang?" He glanced at her. "A real gang?"

Mackenzie shrugged. "They've always hung out together. I don't know what they do exactly, but everyone calls them a gang."

Justin took that in. "She ever done a drive-by before?"

"Not like that."

He rocked Hope, who had begun to turn into a sleepy, content baby again. Mackenzie changed Haven, slipped her into bed and picked up Holly. One more to soothe. "I'll ask her not to do it again."

"I will. Thanks."

She met his gaze, her eyes determined. "You know, it's okay to accept help," Justin said.

"I appreciate your offer. But I know what Daisy wants, and I need to tell her she's not going to get it."

He could respect that. Still he wanted to protect Mackenzie and her babies all the more. "If you sell, won't she get this place eventually?"

"It's her father's conglomerate." Mackenzie stood, rubbing Heather's back with a hand to calm her. "Mr. Donovan is well-known to play dirty to get what he wants. He and his partners have made so much money chewing off the best parts of BC that they think they're invincible. I won't sell to them."

"Won't he just send in a dummy buyer?"

Mackenzie looked at him. "I'll figure it out."

He nodded. She would; she'd think of something.

"Then again," Mackenzie said, "I've been giving serious consideration to the suggestions you and the other guys have come up with."

"Yeah?"

She came to him, and, still holding the baby, leaned down and kissed him a sweet, hot one on the mouth. "Yeah. What do you think about that?"

He swallowed hard. Told himself it was time to face his future. Bad knee and all, he could handle this family. This amazing woman was basically saying she saw them as something of a partnership.

"I like it," he said, pulling her and the baby into his lap next to Hope. "I like it a lot."

Chapter Eleven

"This was just delivered to us by courier," Suz said the next morning, waving a large brown envelope at Mackenzie. "Or should I say served?"

A little ice slid down Mackenzie's back at the word *served*. "Who is it from?"

"A Dallas law office." Suz tore it open. "What do you know? It's a love letter from the Donovan Corporation, and your dear ex, Tommy. They have formed a dubious partnership to take over the ranch."

"How can they?" Mackenzie went to stare over her sister's shoulder.

"Because you were married to Tommy," Suz said, studying the papers. "Apparently, he feels entitled to half the ranch, which he wants to sell to the Donovan Corporation, Daisy's father, in essence."

"He never owned half the ranch," Mackenzie said. "It wasn't in his name. And nothing came up about it in the divorce proceedings."

"Therein lies the rub." They sat down on the sofa together. Suz and Mackenzie glanced up when Justin walked in. "You're just in time," Suz said. "You might as well enjoy the next phase of the thrilling saga, Hanging H Tough, since this concerns your employment."

"It's nothing," Mackenzie said quickly.

"It's something," Suz shot back. "We're being sued by your pinheaded ex and Daisy's greedy father."

Justin sat down across from them. "Can I help in any way?"

"Well, I guess you could marry my sister," Suz said, still staring at the papers.

"Suz!" Mackenzie shook her head. "I don't think that will help. Please excuse my sister, Justin. Sometimes she has a mouth problem."

He grinned. "I'm okay with little sister."

"It says here," Suz said, "that we're behind on taxes. Is that true?"

Mackenzie's mind raced. "I don't think so, but I was in the last stages of my pregnancy at tax time, so there's a chance it slipped my mind." Horrified, she pulled out her laptop to check her records. "I guess I didn't pay them. But we're still in the grace window. I just have to pay interest on what I owed, which is a bummer but not the end of the world."

Suz looked up. "Which means Daddy Donovan has someone working in the records office if he knows we're behind by a couple of months. Dirtbag."

Mackenzie took the paperwork from her sister. "So I'll go down and pay them right now."

Suz hopped to her feet. "I'll go with you. In case there's any trouble."

"No. You stay here with the babies, if you don't mind." The last thing she needed was Suz raising hell in the tax office.

Justin stood. "I'll drive you."

She met his eyes, grateful for his calm, nonjudgmental strength. "Thank you."

"Please pop someone for me, Justin," Suz said, "if they

give my sister any trouble. She's far too nice for her own good."

He laughed. "No popping will be necessary. Just a check will probably solve the whole matter."

"And then Daddy Donovan can shove this silly suit right up his—"

"Suz." Mackenzie grabbed her purse, making sure her checkbook was inside. "The babies will be up any second, but Jade and Betty are on the way. I'll be back in an hour."

"Take your time," Suz said cheerfully. "The girls and I will hold down the fort. When they wake up, we'll have a long chat about how they're not to ever fall for Daisy's— or anyone's—baloney. They have to be Hawthorne tough."

Justin walked Mackenzie to his truck and opened her door for her. "Your sister doesn't pull her punches."

"She never has. She's serious when she says she'd pop Robert Donovan a good one. And nothing good can come of spitting in your enemy's eye." She wasn't being entirely honest—she was so steamed with Tommy right now that were she to run across him, she certainly would pop him a good one. The man had no scruples. The fact that he planned to rob his own daughters' of their birthright inflamed her.

"You're quiet. You sure you're all right?"

She tried to gather her temper into a neat, tidy ball. "I'm furious, to be honest."

"You're quiet about it. Suz is loud." He reached for her fingers, held them in his warm, comforting hand. "Maybe her idea is worth considering, Mackenzie."

"What id— Oh, no, Justin. Suz was teasing about us getting married. Actually, she was being annoying." Could this get any more embarrassing? She didn't think so. He clearly felt her circumstances were so dire that he had to sacrifice himself, which was noble, but he didn't know that she could survive the Donovans. "You working at the ranch is enough. Everything else you're doing is beyond the call of duty. Please don't let all the Bridesmaids Creek fun and games get to you."

He released her fingers after a moment. Didn't say anything. Mackenzie looked out the window, her hands tight on her purse, furious with Daisy and Tommy more than Mr. Donovan. Daisy and her gang riding through the ranch last night, deliberately trying to create a ruckus and wake the babies, had been the last straw.

She wasn't going to put up with being harassed out of the home that was her daughters' birthright—if they wanted it.

Of course they would—they'd love growing up at the Hanging H just as she and Suz had.

"The Donovans and Tommy Fields aren't getting my house," she said, and Justin laughed.

"That's my girl."

Mackenzie blinked. His girl? How did that work? Wasn't he Mr. Never-Settle-Down? "I hope you know what you're letting yourself in for."

He wore a confident, amused smile just shaded by his cowboy hat, and Mackenzie slid her fingers back into his, just to let him know he'd best beat a hasty retreat now while he had a chance.

His fingers tightened on hers.

SUZ SAW FROG and Co. across the way, and since Jade and Betty were already in the house cooing at the babies, she struck out to chat up Frog. That man had the wrong idea if he thought he was going to bark up Daisy's tree. The long, tall, sturdy cowboy appealed to her, and, one day, she planned to steal a kiss from Rodriguez Grant. "Hi!" she yelled, waving at the men so they'd stop. They turned, and

Frog headed her way—just as Daisy's motorcycle ripped up the drive. She pulled between them, parked her bike, got off and removed her helmet.

She was grinning at Frog with a sassy smile. "Hello, Francisco Rodriguez Olivier Grant," she said, and something inside Suz hit the boiling point. She leaped onto Daisy, pushing her down, and the two of them rolled over and over in the dirt.

"Chick fight!" Squint hollered.

"It's not a chick fight until they start pulling hair," Sam said, but Suz was too busy trying to grind Daisy and her dumb lawsuit into the ground to care. Suz was small, but she was tough—the Peace Corps had focused her—and there was no way Daisy was getting up until her hair was full of twigs and dust and her chamois skirt with the fringe was a darker shade.

She felt Frog pulling her off Daisy and she fought wildly to shake him off. "What are you doing?"

"Keeping you from going to jail, tiger." He set her on her feet behind him and let Squint help Daisy up, which Squint was only too glad to do by the mesmerized expression on his face.

"Ladies, ladies," Frog said.

"Oh, shut up!" Daisy said, abandoning all pretense of being a delicate flower. She glared at Suz. "What the hell was that for?"

Suz grinned at the mess she'd made of Daisy. "For waking the babies last night when you rode through here with your band of rowdies. Next time you pull that stunt, I'll pick you off with a well-placed BB—"

"Now, now," Frog said, covering her mouth with his hand and pulling her toward the house. "You have a nice day, Miss Daisy. Suz can't play anymore."

Suz ripped his hand off her mouth. "Have you lost your

mind? That bimbo's suing my sister and me! The least I can do is make her think twice about what she's doing!"

Frog gazed at her admiringly as he dragged her into the house and into the kitchen. He retrieved a wet paper towel and proceeded to wash her face. She snatched the towel away from him. "Stop babying me."

He smiled. "I haven't babied you yet. You'll know when I do—and you'll like it."

She sighed. "You're so full of horse pucky. You had no right to stop me from doling out some just deserts on Daisy."

"I can't have you going to jail, cupcake. And that little lady is the type to press charges. You know what would happen if you went to jail?"

"I'd go to jail," Suz said, annoyed.

"And it would break my heart," Frog said.

She blinked. "Full of crap, Rodriguez."

He laughed. "You'll never know, love, unless you find out."

She had no intention of falling for his cowboy blather. "You can show yourself out."

"Yes, ma'am."

He did so, and Suz crept to the kitchen window to watch him walk away. The fellows were still standing around talking to Daisy, who was no doubt whining about the ever-so-tiny can of whup-ass Suz had uncorked on her.

Baby.

She was relieved to see Rodriguez walk a wide circle around Daisy and go into the bunkhouse.

"Smart man." *And a smart man is right up my alley.*

JUSTIN WAS AFRAID Mackenzie was in over her head with the Donovan/ex-husband problem. Nothing good could come of the deck being stacked against her to that extent, and from the sound of things, there couldn't be a much worse posse to be after the Hanging H.

He waited while Mackenzie paid the tax bill, noting her relieved expression when she came out of the courthouse. "It's paid."

"Sorry you had to go through that." He helped her into the truck.

"It was embarrassing but nothing more." Mackenzie smiled at him. "Thanks for driving me."

He didn't say he wanted to be around in case there was a problem. His suspicion was that merely paying the tax bill wasn't going to be enough to stop Donovan and Tommy from teaming up to get Mackenzie and Suz's ranch. Back taxes had been the first look into how vulnerable the Hawthornes were. They'd find another crack to try to wedge open.

Very bad to have greedy takers in cahoots against you.

"You're going to need to consider legal counsel of your own," he said quietly, steering the truck toward the ranch.

"You think this won't be the end of the lawsuit?"

"I think that you're in a vulnerable spot and they're going to try to exploit that."

"Excuse me, but I don't feel particularly vulnerable."

He smiled. "That's good."

She sighed. "Oh, who am I kidding? You're right. The Donovans are known to be ruthless, and God knows Tommy is dumb enough to go along with anything if there's a buck involved."

He shook his head. "Wrapping up the estate for you and Suz would be a good idea. Do you have a will?"

"I'll call a lawyer. Get everything done." He felt her perk up beside him. "Monsieur Unmatchmaker will know who would be good in this situation."

He wished he felt comfortable about her asking legal

advice from someone who billed himself as an unmatch-maker, but that was hardly his business. Mackenzie was vulnerable right now—any new mom would be, never mind a mom of quadruplets holding down a ranch basically on her own—but she also had a strong sense of independence. He was pretty certain she wouldn't appreciate him putting too much of his nose into her business until—if and when—she asked. She'd been recently burned by her divorce, and he didn't figure Mackenzie was all that interested in being overly advised by a man.

"Hey, what's Daisy doing here?" He pulled up the drive, surprised to see Daisy with Squint and Sam.

"Being her typical man-magnet self." Mackenzie hopped out of the truck. "Daisy, hit the road. Get off my property before I file a restraining order against you."

Justin switched off his truck right in the drive and strode after Mackenzie, whom he sensed was in no mood to be baited by Daisy. Mackenzie waved the brown envelope containing the lawsuit at Daisy.

"This isn't going to work," Mackenzie told Daisy. "I paid my tax bill. You're not going to get my ranch."

"You paid it?" Daisy looked at Justin. "Did he loan you money?"

Justin saw Mackenzie take a deep breath to contain her temper.

"Why would my employee need to loan me money, Daisy?" Mackenzie demanded.

"Everyone knows you're dead broke. Anyone would struggle with four kids. So it stands to reason—"

"Daisy, go away. Right now. I very seriously will file a complaint against you—what happened to your face?"

Justin had wondered the same thing.

"Your crazy sister happened to my face." Daisy looked to Squint and Sam for confirmation, and both men nodded.

"Suz?" Mackenzie headed toward the house.

"You put a muzzle on Suz, and I won't file charges for physical violence, whatever it's called," Daisy called after her. "I've got three witnesses."

Mackenzie turned around, marching right back to the group. Justin steeled himself in case he was needed to protect Daisy.

"If you file anything against my sister," Mackenzie said, "you will wish you hadn't, Daisy."

"Why?" Daisy asked. "You have nothing. My father can buy and sell you all day long."

"And you think life is all about money?" Mackenzie asked.

Silently, Justin applauded this. "You'd best go, Daisy. The Hanging H is closed. You're trespassing."

Daisy glared at Justin. "I'll go, but this isn't the end of anything. Not by a long shot, Mackenzie."

Justin winced. Bad combination: Daddy's money and a spoiled brunette.

Daisy glared at all of them before she hopped on her motorcycle. "See you later, Squint, Sam."

He hauled ass after Mackenzie, who was long gone. Justin found her in the nursery, her hands on Suz's face, staring at the scratches on her sister's cheeks and arms.

"I just saw Daisy," Mackenzie said. "It looked like you won."

Suz looked pleased. "Never doubt it."

"Here's the thing," Justin said as Mackenzie hugged her sister. "I'll do the fighting from now on."

"You're a mom," Suz told Mackenzie before turning to Justin. "And you're not family. I'll do the fighting for the Hanging H."

"The next fight is going to be in a court of law." Mackenzie forced Suz to sit in a rocker. Smiling at her babies, she lifted Holly out of her crib when she started to stir. "Justin says we need to get some legal counsel, make certain everything is tied up tight."

"All of my portion can go to the girls," Suz said.

Mackenzie gasped. "Absolutely not!"

"It's not like I'm ever going to have kids." Suz glanced at Justin. "While the stork may not be finished visiting you."

Mackenzie blushed, which Justin thought was cute. She didn't look his way.

"Give me Holly," he said, reaching for the baby. "You girls have a lot to talk about. Holly and I will take a walk."

"There's no need." Mackenzie looked at him. "We're not talking anymore today. Suz needs to call up some friends and get out of the house for a change. Be a young person."

"I'll take care of your sister," Justin told Suz. "I agree with Mackenzie, though. I wouldn't make Daisy's life too miserable. We don't want her figuring out a way to have you arrested."

"The sheriff is a family friend," Suz said. "That's why the Donovans went straight to a lawsuit. They knew the sheriff's office would never bring any non-serious complaints to us. The town has been evenly split for a long time, with most folks siding with us instead of the Donovans. It chaps Daddy Donovan's big-bucks ass."

He looked at Mackenzie. She studied him for a minute, reached out to take Holly back. "You go, too."

Justin wasn't going anywhere. "I'd rather stay, if you don't mind."

Suz slipped out of the room. "I'm going into town," she called back down the hall.

"Suz is right," Mackenzie said. "You shouldn't try to fight our battles."

Justin shrugged. "I'm not fighting anything. But I'm here should you need anything."

"You've done enough." She kissed the top of Holly's head, and Justin felt something tug at his heart. "We weren't looking for a knight in shining armor."

"Well, I'm no knight, and I wouldn't be caught dead in medieval armor." He glanced around the room at the babies suddenly stirring. Heather tried to roll over without much success—she was too young for that but she gave it her best shot, craning her neck around—Haven blew a bubble, then spit up, which Mackenzie was quick to wipe away, and Hope looked like she was about to let rip an ear-stunner. "You're sure you want me to go?"

"Yes." Mackenzie nodded, juggling burp cloths and babies. "We'll manage."

He had no doubt of that. Still, he cruised down the hall into the kitchen to give her privacy but to remain within earshot in case baby pandemonium hit a freakish level. But all sounded calm down the hall: infant wails were addressed, and he could hear Mackenzie singing and cooing to her babies.

Maybe she didn't need him. Actually, he knew she didn't, but he was hoping he fit somewhere in her life.

Mackenzie had a lot on her plate. Perhaps the best thing to do would be to give her some space. He understood needing space—if he didn't, he'd be in Whitefish right now, on his father's ranch, taking over the family business. There was no reason to do that, not with three other able-bodied brothers who were more interested in it than he was, even if the old man said Justin was his top choice to take over.

Sometimes space was necessary.

He left the house, closing the door quietly behind him.

MACKENZIE WAS STARTLED when the front doorbell rang, since everyone always used the back door and most people walked right in, anyway. So it couldn't be Jade or Betty, or even Daisy, who used the back door as if she were one of the close-knit circle that visited the Hanging H. Casting a quick eye over the babies to make certain they were all secure for the two minutes she'd need to be gone, Mackenzie picked up Hope and took her to the door with her.

"Who is it?"

"Robert Donovan."

"Lovely," she said to Hope. "Gird yourself for the first true annoyance in your young life." She pulled the door open. "I thought you do all your talking through a lawyer."

Robert Donovan cast a tall shadow, and he wasn't a particularly friendly-looking character, either. He had buzzed short hair—too impatient to be bothered with combing it, she supposed—and a self-righteous smirk.

"I should have called on you sooner," Robert said. "Instead of sending my request through my lawyer, for which I apologize and hope to make amends. May I come in?"

"Absolutely not."

"It's difficult to discuss what I have to say standing on the—"

"Mr. Donovan, I have four babies. I don't have time for this. Say what you came to say."

His smirk widened. Mackenzie stared at him, wondering if the man might be an idiot. She was two seconds from slamming the door when he sighed.

"I'm an old man, Mackenzie."

"That sounds like a personal problem to me."

He laughed. "Indeed. But old men like to build kingdoms."

"All well and good, but not my problem." She glanced over her shoulder, wondering if she'd heard something.

One ear stayed cocked to listen for the babies. In her arms, Hope stayed very still, gazing out into the sunlight, which tall Mr. Donovan mostly obscured. "Can you get to your point?"

"I'll send all four of your daughters to private colleges or university, and pay twice the offer I made you on your property, if you agree to sell it to me by September."

"This September," Mackenzie said flatly. "Less than thirty days."

He nodded. "I'll buy all your equipment, horses and so on. And I'll buy whatever house in town you would like, in your name, if you're out before the end of September."

She'd been wanting to sell, hadn't she? Said she would? It was a generous offer, more generous than any she'd ever get for the Hanging H most likely. "What makes you think the Hanging H is for sale?"

"I heard in town you're not interested in reopening your family's business and that you've got your hands too full to run the place. Noticed you've hired on new hands." Robert shrugged. "Wanted to see if I could help you out. As you may know, I'm a generous man where Bridesmaids Creek is concerned. I try to be very civic-minded."

"If you're so generous, why didn't you make me this offer instead of roping my ex into a deal with you?"

Robert smiled. "Actually, Mr. Fields contacted me on the matter."

Mackenzie's body tightened to perfect stillness. Hope bobbed a little in her arm. "It was Tommy's idea to file the lawsuit?"

The big man shrugged. "I generally prefer to work things out in person. Mr. Fields seemed to believe that as you'd parted on poor terms, as I believe he put it, the professionalism of legal papers would be a better instrument to conduct business."

That rat bastard. No scruples at all at trying to take his own daughters' inheritance.

"Mr. Donovan, the Hanging H isn't for sale. I'm not overwhelmed, contrary to what you might have heard." Mackenzie took a deep breath. "You're not the only one who likes to help out Bridesmaids Creek. My family spent many years building up this town, as you know, even though you only came here when Daisy was what? Two, three years old?"

Robert Donovan hated to be reminded that he wasn't born and bred BC, despised knowing that the town still considered him an outsider in spite of his money and the weight he liked to throw around.

"Daisy and Suz were in class together," Mackenzie said. "I remember it well when she came to the haunted house that year. She was afraid of the puppets, and one of the chickens pecked her finger and made her cry. City girls don't see that many chickens, of course, and she didn't know not to pull its feathers. But she's grown up a lot since then." Mackenzie kissed the top of Hope's head. "I do appreciate you stopping by and discussing your offer in person." She shook her head. "But if I were you, Mr. Donovan, I'd avoid doing business with Tommy Fields. No matter what he tells you, I'm difficult to deal with on any terms, whether legal instruments or face-to-face."

He looked frozen, not certain how to proceed.

She took another deep breath. "And the Haunted H will be open for business by October, so you're welcome to spread that news all over Bridesmaids Creek."

Mackenzie closed the door and walked into the kitchen, where she knew Justin would be sitting.

"I knew it was you I heard," she said. "Eavesdrop much?"

"I eavesdrop a lot, particularly when black Bentleys pull into your drive." Justin grinned. "Opening the Haunted H, huh?" He reached out to take Hope from her, snuggled her in his arms. "Your childhood just changed, sugar. You're going to grow up with a mother who runs a haunted house. How cool is that?"

Mackenzie shook her head and went to check on the other babies.

Cool? He had no idea.

Chapter Twelve

"I don't know what got into me, but I know it's the right thing to do, if all of you believe it's a good idea to bring the Haunted H back," Mackenzie told the people gathered in her kitchen. "I realized that this ranch isn't just mine—it's Bridesmaids Creek's, too. A lot of people have happy memories of this place, and I want my daughters to share those, as well as your children and grandchildren."

She pushed away the only bad memory she had of the Hanging H and looked at Frog, Sam, Squint, Suz, Jade, Betty and plenty of other townspeople who had showed up for the meeting.

"We'll all help," Jane Chatham said. "Let's open on a Sunday night, when our shops and diners are closed in town, so we can all be here. I, for one, look forward to celebrating the grand opening!"

"Good idea," Madame Matchmaker said. "Let's start small, get our feet wet. Not overpromise at first. It took your parents years to get the Haunted H built up to being the best children's harvest fun around."

"Agreed. Good idea." Mackenzie nodded. Suz grinned, delighted by Mackenzie's change of heart, and waved Haven's fist at her mother. Justin held Hope, Monsieur Matchmaker had Heather tucked into his arms and, for some reason Frog had ended up with Holly. Since Frog was wedged in as tight to Suz as he could get, maybe it wasn't all that surprising he'd ended up with a baby.

"What about the dead man?" Daisy's voice called from the back. "No report was ever filed on how he died. How do we know that doesn't happen again? It was a real black eye on Bridesmaids Creek, and we don't want another, bigger, black eye."

The room went deathly silent. A dark cloud seemed to rush past Mackenzie's eyes. "Why would anyone else die here?"

"We never knew what killed him. Could have been food poisoning. Could have been murder," Robert Donovan said.

Since she'd opened the meeting to anyone in BC who might be interested in learning more about the Haunted H reopening, Mackenzie wasn't all that shocked that the Donovans had showed up. Justin winked at her, fortifying her resolve.

"Food inspections are done routinely. It wasn't food poisoning."

"I'll say it wasn't!" Jane Chatham hopped to her feet. "Since my restaurant provides fifty percent of the food that comes to the haunted house, I sure hope you're not accusing me, Daisy Donovan!"

"Nor my cooking," Betty Harper said. "If Jane does half, I'm sure I contributed around twenty percent. Most of my ingredients are organic or grown by me and prepared by me." She stared around the room. "There's not a person in this room who has ever complained of food problems from my cooking!"

"Someone killed him," Robert said, throwing his weight around as usual. "And it didn't take too much digging to find out that the cause of death was undetermined on the death certificate."

"How would you know?" Sheriff Dennis McAdams said. "Death certificates can only be ordered by the family. Cause of death is private."

Robert sniffed. "Reporters dug that information up, Sheriff. Be fair. You've been covering for the Hawthornes long enough."

Mackenzie frowned. "Excuse me, no one covers for the Hawthornes. We pull our own around here."

"You're just mad," Suz piped up, "because we won't sell to you. Isn't that harassment or something, Sheriff?"

"There's probably a good case for it." Sheriff McAdams looked unimpressed by the Donovans' claim. "That man who died here was an out-of-towner, an unfortunate soul with no kin to claim him. The autopsy revealed nothing. Not sure what you're working at, Robert."

"Just saying that there was a stain on this place ever since that day, and everybody here knows it." Robert sat down, pleased with the trouble he'd caused.

"Anyway," Mackenzie said, refusing to let him get to her. "I want to open this to a vote. No one has to like the idea or participate. I'm doing this for my daughters, but if our town doesn't like the idea, if it no longer fits the needs of Bridesmaids Creek, I'm just as happy to be simply a mother and not the owner of an amusement park."

"All in?" Sheriff McAdams asked, and all hands went up but the Donovans' and their cronies'.

"Fine, fine. We're back in business, friends," Sheriff Dennis exclaimed.

Mackenzie met Justin's gaze, startled to see him smiling at her as he'd abstained from the vote. She'd expected that—he wasn't from here, and no matter what he said, he might not stay—but she felt his support, and it warmed her.

After the guests left, Justin waved and headed out the

back door, as well. She hated to see him leave as she peeked out the window at him. Watched Daisy accost him, doing her best to crack his armor. Justin shook his head at her before he headed into the bunkhouse.

Daisy turned around, catching Mackenzie spying on her. Daisy glared and Mackenzie waved cheerfully, then went to check on her babies, still smiling.

JUSTIN WALKED INTO the bunkhouse, his mind completely on the meeting that had just been conducted and the warmth he'd realized the town felt for Mackenzie and Suz. Favored daughters, for sure.

He'd never been a favored son, so seeing it in real life made him a little wistful for the family situation he didn't feel that he'd ever had—except for rodeo. Rodeo had been a different kind of family, but it had been all he'd had. It had sufficed.

Ty walked into the bunkhouse, slapped him on the back. "Mooning?"

"Have you ever known me to moon?" Justin demanded, returning the greeting. "Why are you here again?"

"BC is my home. You know that. I came to check on the boys." He glanced around. "Where is everyone?"

"Off working or finding trouble." Justin didn't really care. Sam, Squint and Frog had proved themselves able and hard workers. He didn't keep too close an eye on them.

"So you're happy with them."

He shrugged. "Sure. I don't think Mackenzie would have reopened the Haunted H without them being here."

Ty nodded. Grabbed himself a beer out of the fridge. "I've got a message to pass along from your family."

"Why?" Justin barely glanced his way. "Can't they call my cell?"

"It was just an offhand thing. I was out there doing some horse trading—"

"Stirring up trouble."

Ty shrugged. "I did need a new horse. And your father and brothers have the best around."

"I don't know anything about that."

"Yeah, you do. You can't go on being the rebel forever."

"Sure I can, if being a rebel means staying away from a place where you're not really wanted."

"Yeah, about that." Ty took a long drink of his beer. "Your dad's not doing too good. He didn't say it, but I think he wishes your mother would at least take a phone call from him."

"Can't help you much, old buddy."

"Justin, it's your dad. If you went home, you could set a lot right."

Justin fell into the nicely worn leather sofa, eyeing his friend. "Look, you brought me here. This was all your idea."

"Yeah, because Mackenzie needed help, and you needed a job. You were never going to rodeo again."

That stung more than it should have. "I'm twenty-seven. You don't know what might happen." He knew exactly what was going to happen. His knee injury was severe enough that surgery might fix it, but there'd be no guarantees of how stable it would be. He'd never rodeo again.

"But getting you on here wasn't a way to keep you away from your family. Now that you're not rodeoing anymore, they'd like to see you."

"You mean now that they've forgiven me for not staying to work the family business?" Justin shook his head. "I'm fine here." He wasn't about to leave Mackenzie and the babies just because his father had decided he finally wanted to acknowledge the prodigal son.

"You might think about it. No one is getting any younger, and you're not exactly barking up Mackenzie's tree. Believe me—I had high hopes on that," Ty said with a sigh. "But things would have happened between you by now if it was meant to be."

"Wait a minute." Justin glared at him. "You don't know that nothing's happened."

"Suz says it hasn't."

Great. Chatty little sis. "Let me worry about my personal life, okay? One thing has nothing to do with the other."

"Okay." Ty gave a melodramatic sigh. "Are you sure you're not bothered by the age thing?"

Justin blinked. "What age thing?"

"You know." Ty waved a hand in grandiose fashion. "You're twenty-seven. Mackenzie's thirty. She's already got four kids and you might want one yourself and she may have had enough of pregnancy."

"You're riding down a ridiculous road right now, bud."

"It all weighs on a man, I'm sure."

"I'm fine," Justin growled. "The reason nothing's happened is because the woman has plenty on her plate. Why do you think she's looking for a husband? To be honest, that seems like the last thing she wants."

"You have to change her mind."

"No, I don't," Justin said. "And you seriously need to butt out."

"All right," Ty said. "Don't say I never tried to help."

"There's help and then there's being freaking annoying."

Ty laughed. "So, Daisy and Frog, huh?"

"I doubt it very seriously. The lady in question is hot

to trot for any man who may look her way. And if I didn't know better, I'd think Frog has eyes for Suz. But what do I know? I'm a cowboy, not Madame Matchmaker." He perked up. "I still think she'd be unhappy if she knew you were operating solo on this gig."

Ty laughed. "I have my marching orders from Madame Matchmaker—believe me."

Justin studied his friend. "Are you saying the two of you are working together?"

"You haven't been in BC long enough to know how things work, but this town is a team, old buddy. And once you're in the team's crosshairs, you're probably going down. Loner, rebel, family issues, financially independent, moody," Ty ticked off. "Then there's hardworking, determined, stubborn, good friend, loyal, daredevil. Catnip around here."

"BC's matchmaking is nothing more than coincidental. No more real than Jane Chatham's fortune-telling." Justin laughed. "Or that business about ladies swimming in Bridesmaids Creek and finding their soul mate."

"Okay, that one's a stretch. It's really just a charity function. But we like to see the gals in their bathing suits. And the week before it happens, we get everybody together to clean up the creek and we test the water. It serves many purposes, so don't critique our ways."

"I'm not." Justin held up a hand. "Just trying to figure out why BC runs so much on lucky charms and rabbits' feet."

"Don't knock it until you try it." Ty went to the door. "Be sure to call your father and brothers at some point. They're ready to hear from you."

He wasn't ready to hear from them.

"Do you know Suz is out there sucking face with Frog?" Ty suddenly whispered.

"I don't care."

He slapped Ty on the back, a brotherly pat, hardly anything at all. Ty coughed and said something about friends shouldn't damage other friend's lungs. Shaking his head, Justin went outside, where he saw Mackenzie loading the van with her babies.

He strode to help her, lifting the carriers into the van, securing seat belts, tucking in blankets. Holly and Haven writhed around, not happy to be stuffed in a car seat and placed backward; Heather looked around at whatever she could focus on. Hope fell right asleep, unconcerned.

"An outing for the girls?" Justin asked.

"Yes. I've taken the idea under advisement that I need to secure my paperwork for my daughters' future." She looked at him. "Now that we've definitely decided to stay."

"I was glad to hear you say it in the meeting." Relieved had been more like it. He couldn't bear the thought of this little family heading off without him, because it was for sure that wherever they went, they wouldn't need a foreman.

Which meant he had some thinking to do. Justin looked at Mackenzie. Her eyes were on him, and all he could think of was how badly he wanted to kiss her.

So he did.

Gently, softly, he kissed Mackenzie's lips, kissing her again and again when he felt her lips moving against his, seeking the same response he was looking for.

Then, to his disappointment, Mackenzie turned away. "I have to go, Justin."

After getting in the car, she switched it on, looked at him one last time and drove away.

She was fighting it hard. That was clear.

But why?

Chapter Thirteen

"We hear that handsome cowboy is living with you," Jane Chatham said after helping her settle the babies in The Wedding Diner. They sat in a quadruple row of darling, and Mackenzie couldn't believe they had a father who wanted to take everything away from them. "Of course, I told everyone that wasn't true," Jane continued.

Mackenzie stared at Jane, stunned. "Why would people think that?"

"Probably because he's a hunk with your name written all over him. Maybe they're hoping for a wedding in this town." Jane smiled. "Most likely, folks want you to be happy. Everyone knows Tommy's been giving you a rough road."

"How is my name written on Justin?"

"I think it's the way he watched your every move in that meeting. He's the real reason you're reopening the place, isn't he?"

Mackenzie shook her head. "My decision is about my daughters. And Suz. I know Suz can take care of herself, but the Hanging H is still her home and she wanted to remain there. Just about the easiest way I know to do that is to do what I know best, running a circus."

Jane smiled. "We'll all help you."

"Thank you."

"But you have powerful enemies in this town," Jane said, her voice suddenly changing. Mackenzie had heard that tone before. An icy premonition tickled at her.

"Enemies who would rather see the Hanging H burn than come back to life," Jane said softly. Mackenzie gasped and grabbed Jane's wrist. Jane jumped, her eyes settling on Mackenzie.

"Gracious! I've left you sitting with no tea and no cake, Mackenzie." Jane hopped up from the booth. "I got so excited to see the babies I forgot about serving you. Please excuse me!"

She hurried off, not taking Mackenzie's order, because she wouldn't have, anyway. But she also didn't remember a word of her warning, because that was how Jane's visions worked. She literally didn't remember having visions sometimes.

But Mackenzie would never forget it. Jane's words slid through her memory like an icy wind. Her premonition was too terrible to contemplate. Surely Daisy and her gang of rowdies wouldn't burn down the Hanging H just to make sure it never came back to its former glory.

But even she knew anything was possible.

Jane set a piece of frosted strawberry cake and a glass of iced tea in front of her. Mackenzie knew she couldn't eat a bite. She sipped at the tea, trying to clear the fear from herself. The babies lay still for the moment in their carriers, and Jane bent down to coo over them.

"You young ladies have no idea how much fun you're going to have as you grow up. It's not many kids who get to grow up in a true haunted house!"

Jane must be wrong. The Donovans didn't want the Hanging H enough to get it by foul means.

She remembered Robert Donovan with his astounding offer to take care of the girls' education, to buy her a home, and she swallowed hard. Jane knew everything. She'd been born here, as her mother and her grandmother had. The names of the first settlers who established and named Bridesmaids Creek were on a stone in the courthouse, and one of those names was Eliza Chatham, Jane's great-great-great-grandmother. "Why do you think Robert Donovan wants the Hanging H so badly?"

"It's very valuable real estate due to its location," Jane said without hesitating. "He's planning big things for Bridesmaids Creek."

Mackenzie sat very still. "Some of which we've managed to thwart."

"Yes, but he's still bought up a lot of Bridesmaids Creek establishments and land just the same." Jane smiled when Holly grabbed on to her finger. "Your ranch just happens to be the crown jewel."

She blinked. "How?"

"Mineral rights, I'd say. You've heard about all the new shale drilling going on." Jane got up. "There's some theory that your land might hold some undiscovered secrets. You should consider making certain the mineral rights to your land are held by you and nothing that Tommy can lay claim to."

"Tommy!" Mackenzie shook her head. "We weren't married long enough for him to have a claim. The divorce is final. He can't sue me for anything." Her mind whirled. "What else should I know?"

"That your cowboy has dubbed himself something of your protector, and that's nothing to sneeze at," Jane said and went off to serve some customers.

Mackenzie looked at the strawberry cake. Beautiful and no doubt tasty as always, but Mackenzie couldn't eat it.

Justin considered himself her protector? She didn't need a protector.

Who was she kidding? She needed all the friends she could get. And a man who really seemed to want to help take care of her ranch—wasn't that almost a fairy tale come true?

DAISY WAS WAITING for her on her porch when she got home. Mackenzie lifted the carriers from her van and set them on the ground, trying hard not to wish that Daisy would simply turn into a toad and hop away.

She came over to help her carry the babies inside instead.

"It wasn't my idea to go after your land when you fell behind on your taxes," Daisy said as she carted Haven inside.

Mackenzie wished she had four arms so she could carry all her babies at once. She really didn't want Daisy near them, though she supposed she was being terribly ungrateful. But Daisy never gave without taking, and what she took usually left you with a painful hole somewhere. "You don't have to help. Thanks."

"I want to. I wish I had a baby." Daisy went back for Heather and set her inside the den beside Haven as Mackenzie toted Hope and Holly. The babies set up a huge wail, Hope spit up and Mackenzie had a strong urge to create a little mayhem herself.

"Look." Mackenzie sighed and tended to Hope's dirty dress. "It doesn't matter about the lawsuit. I'm just back from my lawyer's office, and the ranch and all its holdings are airtight and in no danger, from your father or Tommy or you. So, if you don't mind, please go away. I have a million things to do, and sparring with you isn't going to be part of the game plan."

Daisy looked at her as she went to the front door. "You

know, when we were growing up, I always wished I was you and Suz. You had everything. You still do."

Mackenzie frowned. "What are you talking about?"

"You had two parents who loved you. A haunted house that was all anybody in Bridesmaids Creek ever talked about." Daisy shook her head. "You and Suz were like princesses."

Mackenzie had certainly never felt like a princess, and she knew Suz would laugh out loud at such a notion. "Your father wouldn't try to buy this ranch just because you want it, would he?"

"Of course not." Daisy shrugged. "Dad doesn't discuss his business deals with me. But I think he'd heard through the grapevine that you wanted to sell. He was trying to help you out, like he would a charity or a struggling business."

Mackenzie's eyes went wide. Suz came speeding into the den, Justin not far behind. He came to stand beside Mackenzie, his warmth comforting.

"It's true," Daisy said. "You Hawthorne girls always had everything."

She left with a lingering, almost inviting, glance at Justin. He looked down at Mackenzie, searching her eyes, gauging her mood.

"Okay, Miss Fussbucket," Suz said, bending down to pick up Holly and comfort her. "Gracious, ladies, the wicked witch is gone. You can all relax and stop crying. Uncle Justin can't stand to see a woman cry."

"That's right," he said softly. "You're not going to, are you?" he asked Mackenzie.

"Of course not." She went to wash Hope up, trying to settle her nerves. Darn Daisy, anyway—always looking for a way to get under someone's skin.

And yet something about her story had rung so true, so honest.

"So what was Daisy doing here?" Suz demanded when she returned with a fresh dress on Hope. "Doing what Daisy does best, showing that the apple really doesn't fall far from the old tree?"

"You need a Daisy alarm," Justin said, bringing baby bottles from the kitchen. "She sat on the porch for an hour waiting on you. I couldn't convince her that you'd gone to visit family in another state."

"Because we don't have family in another state," Suz said. "Nice try. Unlike Daisy, we've been in BC since we first saw daylight."

Mackenzie sat on the sofa and picked up a bottle to start feeding Hope. "I think that's part of Daisy's problem. She claims she was always jealous of us."

"The girl who has it all? I doubt it." Suz plunked down with Heather and grabbed a bottle from Justin. "Don't let her work on you. You know that's what Daisy does best, gnaw away at something until it finally cracks."

Mackenzie smiled at Justin as he carried Holly to the window to check the front of the house. "We could turn the tables on her. Include her."

Suz's jaw dropped. "Include her in what?"

"The planning and setup for the haunted house. Put her in charge of a committee." Mackenzie caught Justin's expression and had a sudden flash memory of his kiss that morning. Jane's words about the handsome cowboy living with her made her look away.

What a silly rumor.

"Jane had a vision while I was at The Wedding Diner today," Mackenzie said, and Justin made what sounded like a scoffing noise.

"Oh?" Suz perked up. "I hope it was a juicy one!"

"You don't really believe in that nonsense," Justin said. "Isn't that just another way to sell Bridesmaids Creek's many tales of make-believe? Kind of like the small towns who rely on their ghost stories and sightings for tourist trade?"

Suz gasped. "Justin! Those are practically fighting words in BC! Our livelihood depends on our small-town charms!"

He looked at Mackenzie, who shrugged. "It was a real vision." There was no mistaking it when Jane went into a trance.

"So? So?" Suz prompted.

"She said the Hanging H is going to burn to the ground," Mackenzie said.

The babies all set up a tremendous wail, despite their bottles, almost like a sudden attack of four-way colic.

"Gosh!" Suz scrambled to grab Haven, who'd been so patient about waiting her turn. "You'd think they knew what we were talking about!"

Justin's mouth was set in a firm line the next time Mackenzie looked up. It had taken a full five minutes to calm the babies, but what Jane had seen still hung in the air, a specter that probably wasn't going to go away anytime soon.

"Look," Justin said slowly, "I'm no expert on BC. But I don't believe in spells or magic or visions. A bull rider might be superstitious, sure, but most of the time he's thinking about winning, not getting crushed under a bull. He can't afford to think about negative karma. I think it's best if you don't let word become deed, in Jane Chatham's case." He shrugged. "Not that my opinion counts for anything."

Suz's eyes were wide. "It is a terrible thought, Mackenzie."

She felt horrible that she'd brought it up. She'd just wanted so badly to get it off her mind, out of her head and into the daylight where it could be laughed away.

It just wasn't a laughing matter.

"It's okay," she said quickly, wanting to soothe the horrified look from Suz's eyes. "I shouldn't have told you."

"Of course you should have," Justin said, crossing back to the window. "Because you can't handle everything yourself. That's what friends are for, to share the load."

"That's right," Suz said. "We can't let Daisy and Jane and other people deter us from our goal, which is to bring the Hanging H back to all its wonderful splendor. I think Mom and Dad would be proud of us, don't you?"

Mackenzie looked at her little sister. In spite of her worldliness, Suz would always be her best friend and her connection to the family they'd once been. Suz was tough, but she could also be that child who tagged along after her big sister looking for reassurance. She remembered the scare when Suz had fallen from a tree, breaking her arm, and the late-night run to the emergency room in Austin when Suz had come down with meningitis. It had been so scary, such a frightening time. Mackenzie had been terrified she might lose her only sibling—the tiny baby her parents had brought home one day and allowed her to name. Betty Harper had come to babysit Mackenzie while her parents had taken Suz to the hospital, and Jade had comforted her, telling her she'd always be her friend.

Mackenzie caught Justin's gaze on her, and she needed desperately to change the subject. "Jane isn't all about visions. She also mentioned some folks in town seem to think you're living with me."

"Oh?" He raised a brow, seemed amused.

"I just mention it in case you're worried about your reputation."

He laughed. "A lot of BC gossip tends to be about this place, doesn't it?"

"It's not surprising when it's a onetime haunted house and one of the owners has four children all at once. Tends to make folks talk," Suz said practically.

He shook his head and turned away. Mackenzie caught him smiling, though. The only reason she'd brought the rumor up was to get his reaction and test that rebel reputation he held so dear.

"Guess I'd have to be pretty thin-skinned to worry about a rumor," Justin said.

"One never knows how a man feels about being the subject of such a rumor," Mackenzie said, knowing she sounded prim.

Suz laughed. "Men love it when ladies talk about them. Justin has all kinds of a reputation in town for being a major ladies' man."

Mackenzie stared at her sister. "How do you know that?"

"Because people don't just gossip about the Hanging H," Suz said. "They also gossip about newcomers. And the newcomers du jour are Justin and the three hunks we've hired on. Justin's right about this place being a gossip factory." Suz kissed the baby she held as she looked at Justin. "I've heard everything from you're married, to you didn't really leave the circuit because of your knee but because your heart was broken by a cheating fiancée, to—"

Suz's teasing words came to a stop. Justin's expression had turned grim. He put his baby gently onto the pallet, astonishing all of them, and walked out of the room. They heard the kitchen door close.

"Gosh! Was it something I said?" Suz asked.

Apparently so. But clearly Justin wasn't about to deny any of the rumors.

Chapter Fourteen

Ty strolled into the kitchen the next day, pretty much grinning from ear to ear.

"Why are you so disgustingly happy?" Suz demanded.

"Life is good. Why shouldn't I smile?" Ty glanced at the four babies Suz and Mackenzie had put in the kitchen in a playpen while they did some baking. It was never too early to begin baking and freezing the treats the Haunted H was known for. "Anyway, I heard the big meeting is being held here today to discuss opening this joint back up."

"You missed it by a day," Mackenzie said, slightly miffed with Ty. The way Justin had lit out last night made it obvious that he wasn't the no-strings-attached bachelor Ty had portrayed him as—which was worrying, since Mackenzie recognized she'd begun falling for her foreman. "How does it feel to know that your usually sterling gossip line has failed you?"

Confusion crossed Ty's face. "The meeting was yesterday?"

"Yes, it was. And we are open for business," Suz said. "Do you want an assignment? We could put you in charge of the petting zoo. Maybe the carriage rides or the toss-the-water-balloon-at-the-clown game. That would be my choice for you."

Ty sank onto a barstool. "You can't reopen."

Mackenzie looked up from diapering Hope. "Why not? Everyone who was here for the meeting voted the idea in unanimously. They're looking forward to bringing tourists back here. Except for the Donovans, obviously. They were 'no' votes, but they don't count."

"I get it," Ty said. "But Justin's leaving."

"We don't need Justin," Suz said. "We can stand on our own two feet."

"What do you mean, Justin's leaving?" Mackenzie demanded, her heart skipping a beat.

"He called last night. Said he was ready to take me up on my offer. I'm here to pick him up. Didn't you know?" Ty asked, looking at her closely.

"Like any employee, Justin's free to give notice whenever it suits him," Mackenzie said, fibbing through her teeth so Ty wouldn't know how stunned she was. She felt Suz's stare on her.

Ty shifted uncomfortably. "He didn't sound too good when he called. He sounded like he had a lot on his mind, needed to unwind."

"Justin's personal affairs are his own business," Mackenzie said, dying a little inside.

"You're not as smooth as I thought you were," Suz told Ty, who looked a little disturbed by this news.

"If you'll both excuse me, and keep an eye on the babies," Mackenzie said, "I'm going to go hunt up my foreman. I'll let him know you're here."

She went out the door, heading across to the barns, anger carrying her boots across the dirt-and-stone path quickly. Justin was in the paddock behind the barn, working with a large chestnut. Mackenzie went up to him slowly so she wouldn't startle the horse.

"Ty's here."

"Great. Thanks." He patted the horse on the neck, praising it for its good work. "Listen, about yesterday, I want you to know that none of that gossip Suz was teasing me about is true."

He walked the horse to the barn, and Mackenzie followed. "Is that why you're leaving? Because of the gossip?"

Justin shook his head. "I'm not going anywhere."

Mackenzie stopped, eyeing him as he hosed the horse down. "Ty says you called him to say you're ready to hit the road again."

Justin nodded. "I'm ready to help him out. But I have no intention of leaving anytime soon." He glanced at her. "Did you think I was leaving? Is that why you came out here with a full head of steam? I could tell by the starch in your march that you were pissed about something. Had no idea it was me." He grinned. "On the other hand, I kind of like the idea that it would matter to you if I left."

"Of course it would matter. You're the foreman."

He nodded. "Okay."

She put her hands on her hips. "Were you testing me? My feelings?"

"No. I think I know what your feelings for me are."

He couldn't possibly know. She didn't even know herself, not anything she could admit out loud, to him or anyone else. "What do you think my feelings are?"

Justin shrugged. "You don't trust a relationship enough to allow yourself to fall into one right now. So just about anything I do, anything you feel for me, won't be enough to change your mind."

Mackenzie caught her breath. She'd expected anything but his stark assessment—which hit so close to the truth she didn't know what to say. She watched as he put the chestnut in its stall. "So you're leaving because of me?"

He came out, peering back in at the horse, who was now munching hay, then turned to face Mackenzie. "Not today, not for a while. But it's for the best."

She stared up at him. "I don't know what to say."

He touched her face, gently stroking a finger down her cheek. "There's nothing to say."

That was also uncomfortably true. Mackenzie nodded. She wished it were different, but he was right. She wasn't in a place right now to fall headlong in love. She couldn't allow herself to do it. There were the babies to consider—if she was going to get involved in a relationship, it would be with a man who would be a good father to her daughters—and there was the ranch to think about.

"It's all right," Justin said. "I understand more than you think I do. And if you want me to leave sooner, I can. No questions asked."

She shook her head. "Of course not. You're an important part of the ranch."

"I'm training my backup as fast as I can," he said, his tone a little teasing, but Mackenzie didn't smile.

"Frog, Sam and Squint are nice and they're hard workers." She looked into his eyes. "I'd like to keep you on as long as you're comfortable staying."

"I'll help out until October. That's when Ty's planning to hit the road looking for recruits."

Ty had done this—he'd brought a man here he knew she might find irresistible. When she didn't fall fast enough, he'd sent three more to sweeten the pot, which had only made Justin seem even more appealing by comparison.

She'd fallen for Justin, whether she wanted to admit it or not.

"Can I ask you a question?" Justin said.

"Sure." She gazed up at him, wondering if it would be

any easier to say goodbye to him in a few weeks than it would be today.

It wouldn't.

"Did you believe any of that silly gossip Suz brought home? That bit about me being married or having a broken heart or something?"

She couldn't look away from the intensity in his eyes. "I didn't know."

"You don't trust me." He touched her cheek again. "I'm sorry that you don't."

It was true—she'd been upset because she'd been afraid something in the rumors meant that he wasn't the man he appeared to be. They'd never discussed personal issues—for all she knew, he'd had a love life he didn't want to discuss. The fear had worried her, slicing into her feelings for him.

She couldn't deny the gossip had hit her hard. Justin was right: she hadn't trusted him, hadn't trusted the love-making they'd shared.

After a long look into her eyes, Justin nodded, turned and walked out of the barn.

Mackenzie went back to the house, the babies and the baking, her heart splintered and ragged.

Squint, Frog and Sam were gathered around the babies on the floor, playing with them and gazing up at Suz, who was too busy rolling out dough to pay attention to their adoring looks.

Suz was totally oblivious to the heartsick look on Frog's—Suz called him Rodriguez only—face. She would never believe he cared about her after she'd seen him out with Daisy. Mackenzie grabbed the basket of cookie cutters and began pressing them into the dough.

"You're stabbing it," Suz complained, removing the heart-shaped cookie cutter from her sister's hand. "It requires a delicate touch, and that's something you don't have today. You can press cookies tomorrow when you're not taking your mood out on the poor dough. You do the sprinkles. And make them colorful and happy, not dark and moody."

"Moody?" Frog said. "You moody, Mackenzie? How can anyone be moody looking at these little princesses?" He cooed at the babies like a pro. Suz stared down at him, astonished.

"Get up, Rodriguez. You're making me nervous," Suz said. "You're sounding uncomfortably fatherly."

Mackenzie smiled until she saw Daisy roaring up the drive on her motorcycle. The men jumped to their feet like a food truck had arrived and hustled outside—except for Frog. He stared at Suz, one brow cocked. Mackenzie held her breath.

"Go on," Suz said. "I know it's killing you, Rodriguez."

"What's killing me?"

Suz put the cookie dough down. "Look. I know they say a girl has to kiss a lot of frogs to find her prince, but I'm not looking for a prince, so you might as well exercise those hunk skills elsewhere."

Frog looked to Mackenzie, who couldn't move, didn't know what to say. After a minute, he shrugged and went out the door.

"What did you do that for?" Mackenzie demanded.

"He was dying to go see Easy Rider," Suz said flippantly.

"I don't think so," Mackenzie said. "Pretty sure you sent him away. Why?"

"Why do you keep pushing Justin away?" Suz slung some cookies into the oven.

"I don't." Mackenzie flicked a few sprinkles onto the cookies and wished Suz hadn't brought that up. "It's none of my business what Justin does with his time off. You, on the other hand, are definitely being courted. I'm sure of it."

"Oh, Rodriguez is just a ladies' man," Suz began, but the back door flew open and Daisy marched in, waving a fistful of papers.

"These are the signatures of all the people here who don't want the haunted house reopening," Daisy announced. "There's over five hundred, and for a town of two thousand, that's a quarter of our population."

"How many fake signatures on that petition?" Suz asked sweetly, snatching the papers from Daisy's hand.

"All real and verifiable. Not everybody thinks that haunted house did great things for this town. Folks are concerned about the traffic, the parking problems, the trash violations, the pollution, the increase in theft as strangers are drawn here." She smiled triumphantly. "Some of us want our quiet little town to stay quiet."

Suz studied the papers. "The first five names on here are just your usual band of rowdies, Daisy. Carson Dare, Dig Bailey, Clint Shanahan, Red Holmes and Gabriel Conyers. Nothing new to see. We'd expect them to back you."

"Keep reading," Daisy said, her tone challenging.

Mackenzie took half the papers from her sister to cast an eye over the names. "Monsieur Unmatchmaker?"

Daisy nodded, delighted to let a little air out of Mackenzie's happy balloon.

"But Cosette is with us," Mackenzie said. "She was at the meeting yesterday and voted for it."

"As you know, those two commonly play on opposite sides. It's what makes their marriage tick." Daisy admired her nails and sat down on a barstool without asking if she was welcome, which she wasn't. That wouldn't matter to Daisy.

Mackenzie's heart sank as she read over the names, re-alizing the signatures were legit and recognizing some of the people she'd never imagined might not be supportive of the Haunted H reopening.

Justin walked into the kitchen, and it was as if someone threw a switch in the room and shined a light on Daisy. "Hello, Justin," she said, crossing her legs to show off smooth skin ending in a sexy pair of white cowboy boots that went perfectly with her carnation-pink sundress.

Justin nodded. "Daisy. Suz. Mackenzie, have you got a second?"

Mackenzie handed the papers back to Suz. "Sure." She followed him out. "What's going on?"

"I just got a call from my brother, Jack. He says my fa-ther's in the hospital with a little summer cold that seems to be settling in his lungs. They're worried enough to call me. Dad's always been strong as an ox, but apparently he's asking for me. This time I feel I need to go."

"I'm so sorry! We'll be fine here. Don't worry about a thing."

He gazed down at her, so strong and handsome her heart beat harder. The first thought that came to her mind was, *What if he never comes back?*

That was silly. Of course he would.

"Are you leaving today?"

He nodded. "I think it's best. The guys are going to take me to the airport."

He was leaving his truck here—a thought Mackenzie found a little comforting. "Can I do anything besides be selfishly hopeful that everything will be fine with your father and that you'll come back?"

He smiled. Touched her cheek. "I can't make any prom-ises."

"I know." What was she, three years old? She felt needy

for even having said it. Justin had mentioned that his father wanted him to take over the family business. If something happened to his father, Justin would have to do what he had to do. "Of course you can't. What time is your flight?"

"I need to leave now." He waved toward the window; she saw Rodriguez loading a duffel bag into his truck. "I was able to catch a flight this afternoon."

It was happening too fast. She tried to think past the sudden realization that the weeks Justin had been at the ranch might be over, felt selfish for even thinking it when he was worried about his father. "Safe travels. I'll be thinking about your father. And you."

Justin nodded. "Thanks."

He looked like he wanted to say something else, but he turned and walked out instead. Mackenzie stood still, waving as they pulled away, Rodriguez driving, Squint and Sam in the back of the cab.

Just like that, Justin was gone.

Mackenzie went back inside. All four babies were wailing up a storm, and the look on Daisy's face was priceless. Suz ignored the whole scene, blithely rolling dough.

"I guess I'll go," Daisy said.

"Now that the guys are gone," Suz observed icily.

"Now that I've explained the situation about how BC really feels about your haunted house," Daisy said. "Not that I enjoy being the bearer of bad news. Goodness, those babies are *loud!*"

She shot out the door. Suz dropped her rolling pin and rushed to the babies. "What good girls you are to chase off the wicked witch! Let Aunt Suz kiss you and hug you darling little things!" She scooped up Heather and Hope, and Mackenzie grabbed Haven and Holly.

"Suz," Mackenzie said, trying not to smile, "did you use my daughters as weapons against Daisy?"

"Darn right!" She kissed the babies' heads as she grabbed bottles of formula she'd been warming in a bowl of hot water. "Are you nursing?"

"Slowly weaning. Four is just about too much for me, and they seem to appreciate the speed of the bottle."

"That's a Hawthorne for you, expediency over everything." Mackenzie and Suz each grabbed bottles, testing them to see if the chill was off. The babies writhed, wailing unhappily.

"I didn't let them howl long," Suz said. "Just long enough to knock the self-righteous smirk off ol' Daiz's face and send her skittering out of here like a roach."

Mackenzie giggled in spite of herself. "A little mean."

"And effective. So," Suz said. "Rodriguez texted me that he was taking Justin to the airport. What gives?"

"Family emergency." It would do no good to worry about Justin; he was a big boy. Still, that was small comfort. "His dad's fallen ill."

"He'll be back," Suz said confidently. They settled the babies into the carriers on top of the kitchen table, sitting them up, each feeding two babies at a time. "Do you realize you're going to have to buy four prom gowns at a time? Save for four college educations?"

"They'll have to work to go to college, of course. But I'll help them all I can." Mackenzie smiled at her daughters. "It's kind of fun to imagine the future."

"Do you see Justin in that future?"

Mackenzie glanced at her sister. "I'm sort of on a day-to-day schedule in my life right now."

"Daisy noticed Justin didn't kiss you goodbye. She was watching, spying like she was in the CIA or something. It was awesome when the babies let it rip because I knew Daisy couldn't stand not being the center of attention." Suz giggled. "I was hoping one of them would have a nice pooey diaper to add to the general ruckus, because I just know Daisy's perfect little nose would have wrinkled up like an accordion." She looked pleased with the image.

"What difference does it make to Daisy if Justin kissed me or not? Why would he have, anyway?" Mackenzie wasn't going to admit that she'd been disappointed he hadn't kissed her, too.

Suz shrugged. "Easy, young ladies. You don't have to suck down the whole bottle at once." She took a napkin and dabbed at their chins. "Kind of figures he might want a little sugar for the road."

Mackenzie had certainly hoped so, and the fact that Daisy had noticed Justin hadn't kissed her was annoying. "You have my permission to tell Daisy and everyone else in BC that the sugar will be waiting right here for Justin whenever he gets back."

"I'll do it," Suz said, with a mysterious little smile. "You can bet I will."

Chapter Fifteen

When Justin returned to Bridesmaids Creek two weeks later, he was greeted like a long-lost hero, a virtual rock star in a small town of folks who suddenly knew all about him and his business. And seemed to think he was getting married.

Cosette—Madame Matchmaker—beamed at him, waving him over from her booth in The Wedding Diner. "Justin! You're back!"

He went to join her, and she practically pulled him into her booth. "My flight got in about two hours ago. I took a taxi out here, thought I might pick up some goodies from Jane." It had been his intention to eat a hot meal, then head to the Hawthorne spread. If he ate now, he wouldn't be tempted to grab something from Mackenzie's kitchen. All of this had seemed like a good idea until he'd been stopped on the sidewalk by so many people inquiring after his father and his family and wondering if he was back for good. And letting him know how very glad they were that he was back.

It was quite suspicious, but it wasn't until Daisy had sidled up to him and said, "So I hear you're practically ready to propose to Mackenzie," that he realized something had gone terribly wrong while he was gone.

"So," Cosette said, her eyes twinkling. Justin steeled

himself, and, sure enough, she didn't sugarcoat it. "Word is you'll not be needing my services."

He sighed. Accepted the cup of coffee Jane Chatham brought him with a nod, wasn't shocked at all when she pushed Cosette over in the booth and plopped down beside her, her eyes eager.

"Did something happen while I was gone?" Justin asked. If anybody knew what was going on, it was probably these two. "There seems to be a consensus of opinion that I'm looking for a bride."

Cosette grinned. "We did hear something of the sort."

Jane nodded. "Yes, we did. What can I get you to eat, Justin? You've been gone so long that I'll be happy to whip you up anything you want. I just know you're ready for some pot roast and mashed potatoes!"

He was getting the full treatment if Jane wasn't just going to put whatever she had in the kitchen in front of him. "That sounds wonderful. Thank you."

She made no move to leave the booth. He sighed.

"I don't know what happened, but I'm not getting married. Nor do I think the lady in question has any interest, anyway." He looked at them curiously. "Mind if I ask what got everyone all stirred up? I've been asked by about ten people when the wedding is just in the five minutes I was on the pavement outside."

Cosette grinned. "Suz told us all about it. She said Mackenzie can't wait for you to get home so she can give you lots of love and affection. That she misses you like a baby misses a tooth!"

Suz. It sort of made sense. "Suz is wrong. And I'm sure Mackenzie's going to give her what for when she hears what her sister's been sharing."

Jane and Cosette looked crushed. "You have no intentions at all?" Jane asked.

He wondered if he was still going to get the pot roast. Or anything at all to eat. "No intentions. I'm betting Mackenzie doesn't want me to have any intentions. Ladies, she's been pretty clear that ours is a professional relationship. I'm sure she's still not thrilled about her ex-husband and not ready to jump into another relationship." He wasn't any happier about it than they were, but he understood why Mackenzie wasn't looking for a new guy in her life.

Cosette and Jane looked so disturbed he knew he'd hit some kind of nerve.

"They weren't married very long," Jane said. "Tommy just did not turn out as expected."

"Yeah, we kind of misfired on that one." Cosette looked really down about it. "I look forward to the day we can erase that mistake from BC's books."

"Tommy was one of your deals? A Madame Matchmaker fix-up? Ty claimed he misfired."

Cosette and Jane's faces remained glum.

"Bridesmaids Creek is a family. One for all and all for one, or at least that's how most of us feel. Anyway," Cosette said, "never mind. Sorry for poking our noses where they weren't wanted, especially since we were really off-base. We don't usually embarrass ourselves this way."

Jane nodded. "We are the souls of discretion and genteel manners, usually. Sorry about that, Justin."

They vacated his booth like puffs of gentle wind. Justin sat alone with his coffee, which was getting cold, and his pride, which certainly was even colder and lonelier. Drumming his fingers on the tabletop, he wondered if the pot roast might ever arrive, figured it wouldn't. The ladies had clean forgotten about him now that he wasn't toting an engagement ring.

Which made him wonder if he should be.

Nah. Mackenzie didn't feel that way about him. She wasn't in love with him.

Was he in love with her?

Justin rubbed at the stubble that had grown during the past couple of weeks he'd been sitting by his father's side. He'd finally shaken off the pneumonia well enough to go home, got strong enough to tweak Justin about coming home to help with the ranch, run the family business. His brothers weren't really interested or suited. One was a fireman, another a big trader who at least kept the books but wasn't up for the running of a spread. Justin could appreciate that. A man either had the land in his soul or he didn't.

Justin did. But the land he felt strongly about was the land where Mackenzie and her babies were. Anywhere—it didn't matter. But he wanted to be with her, whether she ever felt anything for him or not.

He realized everyone in the diner was staring at him, curious, having already gotten the word from Jane and Cosette—however gossip was communicated here, either by osmosis or by superfast BC grapevine, he didn't know. Didn't matter. He could tell by the gawks and sympathetic—sometimes disappointed—faces that he wasn't the homecoming hero come to sweep their princess off her feet that they'd been hoping he was.

Still no pot roast, either, and he wasn't getting any. Justin stood, nodded to the diners who suddenly weren't staring, left a couple of dollars on the table for the cold coffee and headed to the Hanging H.

MACKENZIE HUNG UP the phone and whirled to face Suz. "Betty Harper just called! She said she heard a rumor in town that Justin's proposing to me when he gets into town, and that people seem to think the rumor started with you!"

Suz's hair stuck up a bit wildly as one of the babies

pawed a tiny fist through it. "I didn't say anything about a proposal, exactly. I just told a few people that you were warm to Justin, warmer than you let on. And that you couldn't wait for him to come back."

"Suz!" Mackenzie was horrified. "Someone will tell Justin when he gets back—you know how BC is! In fact, someone will probably congratulate him on our upcoming wedding!" She gasped. "Or, worse, they might start planning it!"

"That's probably already happening," Suz said. "You know that BC believes in wedding preparedness. Keeps the threat of elopements at bay. We're nothing if not a man-friendly town, and weddings are celebrated like ancient Roman feasts."

"You just can't do that," Mackenzie said. "You can't stoke the gossip pot on purpose."

"But it's so much fun. And it was worth it to see the look on Daisy's face. Oh, if you could have only seen it, Mackenzie. It was like watching a cake fall." Suz giggled, not sorry at all. "I believe in stretching the truth when necessary."

Mackenzie looked down at Holly, who somehow tugged a smile out of her no matter how upset she was with Suz at the moment. "It accomplished nothing. I'll be surprised if Justin even comes back to the Hanging H." She kissed her baby's head, then smiled at the other three. "I love these babies so much. It's hard to think about anything bad happening when I'm with them."

"What will you do, though, if Justin has to go back to Montana permanently?" Suz asked, her eyes round.

The sound of a motorcycle ripping up the drive stopped the practical answer Mackenzie had been about to make. The back door flew open.

"Ha! You think you're so smart," Daisy told the sisters.

"You put out a rumor that Justin is taken, that he's even altar-bound. But funny thing," she said triumphantly. "He was in town today, and he specifically told Cosette and Jane that he has no intentions whatsoever of getting married. To you," she said to Mackenzie. She took a second to let that sink in. "Which means the field is wide, wide open, because if he's back, and you haven't even seen him yet, and the first place he went once he got back was into town, he's not too worried about returning to the Hanging H." She grinned. "Which also means that since he's been living here for a couple of months, and you've had him all to yourself, and apparently have made no impression whatsoever, you won't mind if I offer him a little bit of my own sugar," she said. She shot Suz's way, "I recall you saying something about your sister being all ready to sugar Justin up when he got back, but, obviously," she said, smiling at Mackenzie, "he's not too excited about *that* brand of sweet."

Suz looked like all the air had been taken out of her. Mackenzie shrugged and handed Daisy Holly. "Burp her, Daisy."

She bent down and picked up Haven from the play-pen, cooing at her.

"Is that all you have to say?" Daisy demanded. "'Burp her, Daisy?'" she mimicked. She patted the baby on the back, making a sour face when Holly did indeed burp. "Peeuw. She smells like day-old bread." She handed the baby over to Suz.

Mackenzie laughed and handed her Haven. "Try this one. Maybe she smells different."

"I am not here to burp your babies," Daisy said. Haven burped like a sailor before Daisy even really got a pat going, spitting up a little on her shoulder. "Okay, I get it.

You were just hoping one of them would do that. Very funny."

"Not really." Suz got up to take Haven, and Mackenzie handed Daisy a cloth so she could clean her dress. "We just press everyone into action who comes into our home. All hands on deck, as they say."

"No, thank you," Daisy said, when Mackenzie tried to hand her Hope.

"You'll like this one. She's friendlier than the other two," Mackenzie said, and, to her surprise, Daisy took the baby.

"She is soft," Daisy said reluctantly, patting her back. "But back to Justin—"

Justin knocked and walked in the back door. Mackenzie thought he'd never looked so handsome—a fact that wasn't missed by Daisy as she twirled close to him with Hope.

"Welcome back, Justin," Daisy exclaimed. "And this little dumpling says welcome back, too!"

Justin smiled and took Hope from her. His gaze locked on Mackenzie, and she felt it right in her gut. Couldn't look away. Wished the two of them were alone in the kitchen so she could—

Then Daisy's words returned her to sanity. Clearly Mackenzie and Justin had been the subject of town gossip, and no doubt he felt awkward about it. "Hello, Justin," Mackenzie said. "It's good to see you."

"It's good to be back."

"Are you back for good?" Daisy asked, sidling nearer to him. "I sure hope so!"

"Depends on what the boss lady says." He flashed a smile at Mackenzie. Mackenzie smiled back, relaxing a little. Maybe Daisy was exaggerating. Maybe the gossip hadn't been on full boil in Bridesmaids Creek.

"You'll never believe what Daisy's father has talked me into," Justin said.

Mackenzie stiffened. "Robert Donovan?"

"Well, if it has anything to do with the Donovans, I'd recommend you steer clear," Suz said, sending a purposefully sweet smile Daisy's way.

"Hush, Suz, let Justin talk," Daisy said, and Mackenzie poured him a glass of iced tea and cut a slice of apple pie, which she put in front of him, taking Hope from him so he could eat. Their hands brushed as she took the baby, and, just for a second, it felt like he felt the same thing she did: a spark.

A very hot spark that was eager to flame to life.

"Robert Donovan says I need to do a run down Best Man's Fork for charity," Justin said. "That's some kind of race thing, right?"

Mackenzie stared at Justin, recognizing at once where this was going. "It's a race."

"Yeah." He nodded. "And the winner gets to donate the prize to the charity of his choice. I thought that was a great idea."

Daisy grinned at Mackenzie, her eyes sly. "There's two prizes, you might say. We have a legend here in Bridesmaids Creek—"

"We have a few legends," Suz interrupted. "Most of them are really superstitions."

"Don't ruin it," Daisy said, wrapping an arm around Justin's. "Suz is a spoilsport. I'm so glad you took Dad up on his offer."

"You would be behind this," Mackenzie said.

"Hush, you," Daisy said. "Justin, did Dad tell you how the race works?"

"I and a bunch of other guys run down Best Man's Fork, which is some kind of magical road here." Justin sipped his tea, ate a bite of pie, then reached to take the baby back from Mackenzie. "It's winner take all, your father says. Donation of five thousand dollars to a charity and a secret prize of some sort."

"The 'some sort' is the kicker," Suz said. "If you pick the right side of the fork in Best Man's Fork, you win. You win because there's a woman waiting for you at the end— if you chose the right path—and you get the trophy, the prize and the woman. Supposedly, anyway."

Justin laughed. Met Mackenzie's eyes. "And if I don't pick the right side of the fork?"

"I'll be really sad," Daisy said. "I'm one of the women chosen this year to give the award. So I hope you run fast and pick the path where I am."

Justin looked at Mackenzie. "Are you handing out the trophies, too?"

She shook her head. "I had my turn. Tommy won that year."

"Jeez." Justin glanced at the other women. "You girls are serious about this superstition thing."

The baby in his arms got a fistful of Daisy's hair and gave it a good jerk. "Ow!" she exclaimed, moving away after disentangling the tiny fingers from her hair. "Like mother, like daughter."

Mackenzie didn't look away from Justin. Shrugging, he took another bite of pie. "I'm not much for superstitions, as I've said before. But I'm willing to play for charity. Frog's going to run, too."

"Rodriguez is running?" Suz's voice rose an octave. "He can't!"

"Why not?" Justin glanced at Mackenzie, his brows raised. "He said he was planning to donate his charity bucks to the pet shelter in town. Said they do good work."

Mackenzie took the baby from him again. "Suz wasn't asked to be a presenter, either."

"Because she's just back from Africa," Daisy said quickly. "She wasn't here when the names were chosen."

"And you want all the men to yourself," Mackenzie said. "Which is totally understandable."

"Yeah, how else are you going to get one unless you rig the game," Suz said. She sighed and got up from the table. "You've been a cheater ever since we were in school, Daisy. You haven't learned a thing." She wandered out, and Mackenzie had a funny notion her sister was going to find Frog. She put the baby in the playpen, not able to meet Justin's eyes anymore.

"I guess I'll go," Daisy said. "I'll stop by to check on you later, Mackenzie."

Mackenzie raised a brow at this sudden show of concern. Daisy smiled at Justin, rubbed his arm and floated out the door.

When she was gone, Mackenzie said, "How's your father?"

"Better. He's going to be fine."

She ate him up with her eyes, wishing she weren't annoyed like all heck that he'd gotten roped into the Best Man's Fork run. Maybe Justin was right: all superstitions were silly.

Bridesmaids Creek lived on its fairy tales and legends. It was a great part of what brought tourists to the town. "It's nice of you to participate in the charity run, but are you needed back home?" She was almost afraid to hear the answer. She steeled herself to hear that his family needed him to return to Montana for good.

"I'm back permanently. Or for as long as you need me here."

Forever. Was that an option? She didn't dare speak it

out loud. Darn Daisy had shaken her confidence with her tale that Justin had supposedly said he wasn't looking for a relationship. "You have to watch out for our small-town functions. They're all designed to get men to our town to settle down." Mackenzie smiled at Justin. "BC is a very man-friendly town—I'm sure you've heard by now. We have the Best Man's Fork run, the Bridesmaids Creek swim, which is guaranteed to bring every hopeful bride a husband in a matter of months, and a few other traditions we cherish."

Justin got up and crossed to her. "I have a tradition I cherish."

Mackenzie stared up at him, aware that he was standing very close to her, in her space. Wished he was closer. Mouth-on-hers close. "Oh?"

"Yeah. And this is it."

Chapter Sixteen

Suddenly Justin's mouth was on hers, kissing her, tasting her as if he'd missed her almost as much as she'd missed him, which wasn't possible. Mackenzie leaned into him, wrapping her hands in his jacket, wishing she could crawl into his arms and tell him how much she'd thought about him, but she let her lips do the talking as she kissed him back.

"You have no idea how badly I wanted to do that," Justin said, drawing back. "I thought Daisy and Suz would never leave so I could."

He smelled like wood and something spicy, felt hot in her hands. Mackenzie's heart raced, shocked by the adrenaline of his unexpected kiss. "Kiss me again. Don't stop."

He smiled. "I plan to kiss you much more, no worries about that. But right now, I come bearing gifts for the girls."

She let him go, though she didn't want to, watching as he went out to his truck, then came back inside with four small stuffed animals. A pink giraffe, a white bunny, a pink-and-white-striped bear and a soft, cream-colored dog, all terry cloth and perfectly sized for the playpen or the babies' cribs. Mackenzie watched Justin "give" each baby her new toy, which entailed placing it beside them in the playpen. She got a little misty—she refused to call it teary—felt herself fall a bit more in love.

"Thank you," Mackenzie said.

"For what?" He glanced up at her but didn't stop showing the babies their new toys. Young as they were, they definitely seemed to know that something new was being introduced into their lives.

"The gifts." She took a deep breath. "And for coming back." That was the greatest gift of all.

He shook his head and smiled. "There was no question I'd be back."

Her heart jumped—there was no other word for it. Everything he was saying was so completely the opposite of what she'd heard from Daisy, which was so like her to spread doom and gloom designed to make you doubt yourself.

But Justin was in her kitchen, cozying up to her babies—to say nothing of the amazing kiss he'd given her—and Mackenzie decided it was time to say exactly what was on her mind. Leave no stone unturned.

"I'm glad you're back. I was worried about your dad—"

"Nah. He's strong as an ox." Justin took a seat on a stool, shrugging. "Surprisingly, it was Dad who told me I should stay right here."

"Really?" She sat across from him, trying not to act like she was starved for another kiss, which she was.

"Yeah. Said I seemed happy. That my job agreed with me. Told him I had four little bosses and they kept me pretty busy."

Oh, God, that sounded good. Drew a smile from her. "The girls keep everyone busy."

"Daisy still causing trouble?"

So he'd noticed. "She goes from wanting to sue me to pretending to be my friend. When everything gets quiet with Daisy, I know a shoe is about to drop. It's all right. Daisy's got her group and her father, and the rest of us work around them."

"I heard about her petition."

"News does travel fast."

He nodded. "I've learned that about this town."

She felt a little warm, not quite a blush, but enough to wonder if he was teasing her about Suz's enthusiastic bragging about Justin and Mackenzie being a hot item. "Yes."

"I have an idea about Daisy."

"Don't worry about Daisy. She's always been this way." He had enough on his mind without having to worry about protecting her from a rival she completely understood.

"I'm not the slightest bit worried. So this fork-to-the-altar gig—"

"Best Man's Fork. It's a road that splits in two. You have to choose which path to take, sort of like Robert Frost's 'The Road Not Taken.'"

"And the gag is that a woman is waiting at the end of one lane, in this case Daisy."

She nodded. "This is what I hear."

"So you wait on the other lane. Make things interesting." He grinned. "Two rivals, two lanes, bachelors running wild for charity? That ought to liven things up for BC, right?"

Mackenzie smiled, aware that he was teasing. "That's the purpose of a manhunting scheme."

He winked at her, and Mackenzie couldn't help smiling back. He was just so darn sure of himself. "Who's in charge of this charity gig?"

"Cosette and Jane usually head it up."

"I'll tell them I want the rules changed to include you. School-yard rivals on the Fork." He got up to put his dishes in the sink. "Things will really get interesting if I should run down Daisy's side."

"Interesting, indeed."

"I have to go put up some feed I bought in town. I meant to get it before I left. Saw Ralph Chatham, by the way. Filled me in on the petition."

"I wasn't going to mention it. It's not important."

"It is if the Donovans are trying to drive a stake through your haunted house." He looked at her. "You wouldn't let them do that, would you?"

She shook her head.

"My guess is at least thirty percent of the nay votes on the petition were coerced."

The sting and hurt she'd felt at reading some of the names—her friends' names—on the petition began to melt away. "Why do you say that?"

"It was just something Mr. Chatham said. He'd received a visit from Donovan, as had Monsieur Matchmaker." Justin went to the door. "All of them received pressure from Donovan."

"Pressure?"

"You know Donovan owns a lot of this town. That's his deal, turn it into Donovan, Texas."

Mackenzie blinked. "How do you find all this out?"

"I talk to people." Justin grinned. "And I know that running a ranch like this isn't a game of bean bags. Small towns have their conspiracies and they pick sides. You have most on your side. Donovan has the money." Justin shrugged. "Money is a powerful tool."

"What a creep." She felt sorry for the people he'd leaned on, all in the name of taking over her ranch.

"Yeah, well, don't let him win. I've got my chips on you."

The back door opened, and Ty strode in.

"I thought I'd find you guys here," Ty said. "Heard you were back and—" He glanced down at the babies. "Is it my imagination or have they grown since I saw them last?"

"What's up, matchmaker?" Justin demanded.

"Matchmaker?" Ty looked confused until he saw Justin glance at Mackenzie. "Oh. I wasn't really playing match-maker. Mackenzie needed help out here—you needed a job. I don't mess with Cosette's deal. That's bad juju."

"Sure," Justin said. "Why are you here?"

Ty glanced around the kitchen, and Mackenzie thought he looked a little wild-eyed, even for Ty. "I just heard in town that Cosette and her husband are getting a divorce!"

Mackenzie's jaw dropped. "That's not possible. You heard wrong. That's a mean rumor."

Ty sank onto a stool, dejected. "It's true. They're having financial problems. Donovan leaned on Philippe. Apparently Cosette didn't know that Philippe had gotten a lien on the store that he owns. It's bad, man." He looked at Justin desperately. "Without Madame Matchmaker and Monsieur Unmatchmaker, this town loses a lot of its magic. You may not believe in superstition, you can laugh all you like at our traditions and Jane's fortune-telling skills and Cosette's matchmaking games, but here we believe in stuff." His voice dropped, and Mackenzie could tell confident Ty was truly shaken. "This town runs on the power of positive thinking, man. You gotta do something!"

"I've got to do something?" Justin asked. "Like what?"

"I don't know. Help me think, for God's sake." Ty ran a hand through his short, bristly hair. "We have to put the magic back in BC or it's all over. No one comes to just another small town, a dot on the map, where there isn't any belief, wonder and magic."

Mackenzie patted Ty's shoulder, cut him a slice of pie

and poured him some tea. "Poor Cosette. This is awful. For Philippe, too." She felt terrible.

"Hard times hit us all," Ty said, more low than she'd ever seen him.

"Are you sure they're filing?" Mackenzie asked, hoping this was just an overblown bit of gossip. Justin's gaze landed on her, and she saw that he looked as concerned as Ty.

"I got it from the courthouse. And then Jane Chatham. Not to mention Daisy." He practically growled the name. "Robert Donovan is going to buy up every inch of retail in our town. I hear he's planning on pressuring the planning and zoning committee to redraw the town square. And when that happens, we're lost. He'll open bars and God knows what else. We'll be nothing but *commercial*," he said, alarmed.

"Take a deep breath. Eat your pie," Justin said. "Let us think."

"I feel awful for Cosette. And Philippe. It makes so much more sense that he signed Daisy's petition."

"And that's another thing." Ty waved his fork. "There's going to be no haunted house this year."

"What?" Mackenzie felt comforted when Justin put a hand over hers for a brief moment. "Why?"

"Apparently you have to have all kinds of new licenses for that. Everything you can imagine. Donovan's got this all figured out. He's prepared to tie up every single permit and license until the day the dinosaurs return. Lawyered up like mad."

Mackenzie shook her head. "He can't do that. One man can't ruin everyone's business."

"Donovan can. He just signed a major deal with a big chain of bars and liquor stores to bring their business here. You can bet there'll be strip clubs and—"

"Stop," Mackenzie said. "You're going to make yourself ill." She felt sick herself. "What can we do?"

"What can we do?" Ty asked rhetorically. "It's David against Goliath." He shook his head sadly. "When word gets out about all this, there really will be no magic left in Bridesmaids Creek, our little town that was built on fairy tales and wedding vows." He sighed deeply and hung his head. "It's going to take a miracle to keep our town from becoming a blot on the map instead of the shining star that it is."

Justin slid his arm around her shoulders and thumped Ty on the back in commiseration. Magic and wonder, belief and superstition wouldn't last long in a town that would be overrun by commercialism in the not too distant future. Mackenzie left Justin's side and went to pick up Hope, who'd begun thrashing and letting out little cries, no doubt disturbed by Uncle Ty's dire tone. Justin picked up Haven, and Ty sighed as he got up to retrieve Heather. "Sorry, baby doll—you drew short straw," he told Holly, but Justin reached in and scooped her up, too. Ty muttered, "Oh, so that's how it's done," and rain started to fall outside, first a slight pitter-patter, then a full-blown rainstorm. Mackenzie told herself that rain brought beneficial gifts.

The thought raised her spirits.

"I'm going to kill him," Ty muttered with dark determination. "Donovan must *die*."

Chapter Seventeen

"Whoa, buddy," Justin said. "It's not that bad. No one needs to die."

"I meant of natural causes," Ty said. "Soon."

"That's not the answer." Mackenzie looked at Justin, and he felt his heart pound. This was why he'd come back—Mackenzie and her daughters. "The answer is finding a way to beat the Donovans fair and square."

Spoken like the resilient fighter she was. Mackenzie had no idea what she was up against. But this was a woman who'd had four children with barely a complaint—he couldn't remember ever hearing her down and out about anything. She just kept rising to meet each challenge.

"Yeah, well, I came back here to win," Ty said. "I brought you here to help, not weenie out," he said to Justin. "You're a rebel, right? So get to rebelling here like you did on the rodeo circuit. By the way, how's the knee?"

Justin sank down on a stool. Mackenzie took the one next to him, cooing to the baby she held but still managing to press against his side, bulwarking him against Ty's idiocy.

It felt great.

"I saw the ortho guy while I was gone. The knee is good as new, for a twenty-seven-year-old rodeo rider, anyway."

"Well, I'd applaud and be happy that you can ride again,

but you're not leaving here, and I'm not hitting the road to hunt up recruits. We're staying right here and helping Mackenzie and Suz beat the Donovans like a drum." Ty stabbed the counter with his finger, emphasizing his point.

"Ty, what exactly do you want Justin to do? How is he supposed to rebel? He's not from here," Mackenzie pointed out.

"Fair point. But sometimes an outsider's perspective is very helpful. Then again, Justin could become one of us," Ty said.

"And how would I do that?" Justin asked, instantly realizing he'd played right into Ty's harebrained game.

"Well, you'd marr—"

"No, he wouldn't." Mackenzie glared at Ty. "Look. I know about the matchmaking ad, Ty. And I know why you really sent Justin out here to help me. You claimed I needed help on the ranch, but you really wanted him to help me to the altar, Ty," she said, and Justin could practically feel her annoyance, "I've known you all my life, and I know your heart is in the right place, but please butt out."

Justin had gone still when he'd realized Ty's best suggestion was that he marry Mackenzie—but he was even more stunned that the idea didn't sound as ridiculous as it should. Shouldn't he be yelling at Ty, telling him marriage was the last thing he wanted?

Except it wasn't.

On the other hand, Mackenzie didn't sound all that warm to the idea—and who could blame her? Her ex had just tried to sue her for her ranch.

"Justin?" Ty said. "You've gotten awfully quiet over there."

Mackenzie didn't want to marry him. He could tell by the way she'd said it. Why did that feel like it cut him off somewhere around the knees?

Justin got up. "I'm fine," he said. He laid the babies gently back in the playpen, nodded to Mackenzie and Ty. "We'll get it figured out," he said. "I'll be back at work tomorrow," he told Mackenzie, and then he headed to the bunkhouse.

JUSTIN REGRETTED RETURNING to the bunkhouse as soon as he opened the door. Frog, Sam and Squint were sitting around with several women, and one of those women was Suz, who sat in Squint's lap.

Which was all wrong on every level, because he knew darn well that if Suz had a thing going for anyone, it was the cowboy she called Rodriguez. He counted nine women and some men he didn't know. The fact that there were various stages of dress in the room indicated some kind of strip game was going on.

He reminded himself that Suz was very young— twenty-three—and she'd just gotten back from a Peace Corps tour in Africa, and he'd been a helluva lot wilder than she was when he was her age. "What the hell?" he demanded, his question directed to his three bunkmates.

"Join us," Sam said, and Justin shook his head.

"I don't think so." He looked at Suz. "What are you trying to do, kill these guys?"

She shrugged. "I didn't put this party together. I'm just livening it up."

At least she was fully dressed or he would have had to mess up his bunkmates big-time for stepping over the line with the boss's little sister. By the clearness of her eyes and the fact that her glass of wine had barely been touched, he figured Suz was a latecomer to the party. "All right, everybody out."

"Hey," Frog said, "we're developing our community relations."

"You dork." Justin jerked a thumb at the door. "Everybody out. If we want to get to know you, we'll do it with our clothes on."

The room vacated with no small amount of grumbling. When it was just his bunkmates and Suz left, Justin said, "We're going to plan how to help Mackenzie. You guys are not going to go rogue by making a play for the female population. And you are not going to encourage them in any of their hijinks," he said to Suz, "because your sister is up to her ass in alligators."

"Aye, aye, Cap'n sir," Suz shot back. "I was over here keeping these guys in line, by the way, not encouraging them."

She'd been keeping a careful eye on Rodriguez, if he had to bet. But whatever story she wanted to tell, Suz wasn't his problem. "Here's what I'm suggesting. This Best Man's Fork dog-and-pony show is something we need victims—I mean, participants—for. So you three are going to run with me." He waved at the three bunkmates who had become his brotherhood, not unlike his rodeo brotherhood, except maybe a little less focused. A little less sane. He took a deep breath. "The four of us are going to do this."

Frog pulled his black T-shirt on. Justin figured he'd gotten there just in time, before more clothes were shed. Squint was only missing a belt, and Sam was missing his hat as he lounged in his chair like he'd been about to throw down a winning hand.

"You can't win," Sam said. "You have a gimp knee." He held up a hand as Justin was about to debate the point. "Speak whatever baloney you wish, and I heard all about you seeing your doc at home. Supposedly." Sam grimaced. "You didn't see a doctor because there wasn't time, and your knee isn't good enough for you to win. You know

Daisy's going to put her band of rowdies up against you. You need us," he said, pointing to Frog and Squint, "to weight this in your favor."

Suz stared at him, her eyes huge. "Tag team? Relay? How are you going to do this if you can't run? The town blue hairs have their rules, and they're pretty tight."

Justin sat down and grabbed their cards to lay out a fork shape on the table. "Your sister will be here," he said, pointing to the ace of hearts.

"Daisy, you mean," Suz said.

"We're going to do this fun run a little differently. Mackenzie will be here, and Daisy will be here." He put the ace of clubs to indicate Daisy on the other fork. "The four of us will be here." He laid the four jacks at the beginning of the fork in the road.

Suz glanced at Rodriguez, clearly weighing whether she wanted him running this race, where he might end up in Daisy's arms. Justin frowned.

"Explain this Best Man's Fork thing to me," he said. "I may not have the full significance."

"It's all about marriage," Suz said. "Every man who's made the run and chosen the proper path that leads to the woman has ended up married to her within thirty days."

"That's not possible," Justin said. The other three men stared at Suz, clearly calculating if making this run could be detrimental to their bachelorhood.

"It's a matter of town record. Go ask Jane Chatham for the book," Suz said. "She keeps a ledger of the date of each event in this town and what weddings may result from said event. She also keeps dates of divorces, in the back of the book, in order to discover if marriages stick or fail after BC's illustrious events."

"And?" Justin demanded, curious. Maybe he didn't want to get involved in something that had a high fail rate.

Suz smiled. "Scared?"

This woman very well could end up being his sister-in-law one day. Justin sighed, raising a hand at her teasing giggle. "Not scared. Looking to be informed. Information is power."

"Two percent."

Justin leaned back. "Two percent of these wedded couples didn't work out."

"Exactly. My sister. It is what it is." Suz shrugged. "They shouldn't have gotten married in the first place."

"Why?" Sam asked. "They had kids."

"Yeah, but Mackenzie was never in love with Tommy." She swept the fork of cards off the table, then shuffled the deck. "Tommy just wanted to marry the town's favorite daughter. Then he spooked because of the babies. No Best Man's Fork, no Bridesmaids Creek swim, can predict whether a man has a chicken side or not."

Justin frowned. Personally he thought the little girls were a huge bonus in his life. He loved those babies. When he'd been in Whitefish, he couldn't wait to get back to them and Mackenzie.

If this was the way things were done in Bridesmaids Creek, then he planned to win. "I don't have a chicken side."

"That I believe." Suz grinned at him. "It remains to be seen how fast you are. I can tell you right now that Daisy's going to be ticked when she finds out you've rigged the game with a fifty-fifty chance by putting Mackenzie in the other fork. Expect a formal protest. However, I'm willing to help you any way I can. Inside the rules, of course."

"Let me get this straight," Squint said. "I don't know why Daisy's using you for this event, because quite frankly, I'd be a more exciting candidate." He glared at Justin. "But if you're planning to secretly put Mackenzie on the other side of the game, I'd carry you on my back to get you over the finish line."

"I can run," Justin said. "Don't worry about me."

Sam looked at him doubtfully. "I guess we could make one of those chariot things. Like a litter or one of those Iditarod thingamabobs with the mush dogs." He grinned at Justin. "We'd drag you up to the finish line in record time."

"Or," Frog said with great bravado, "we'll run the race to the finish line just to secure the win, then double back and get Justin."

Justin laughed. "Double back and get me?"

"We won't let you down, bud," Frog said earnestly. "We won't let anyone else get your girl."

"Get my girl?" Justin's brow wrinkled. "That's not what this is all about. I'm trying to support Mackenzie. And Suz and the Hanging H. Bridesmaids Creek, in general." He raised a brow at Suz's giggle. "I'm protecting her against the Donovans."

"And what if you win the race and Mackenzie is in the fork you choose? Are you prepared for what happens in thirty days or less?" She gave him a Suz smirk. "I should warn you that some of the participants just went ahead and eloped that very night, as soon as the race was completed."

"Whoa," Frog said. "Maybe I don't want to run. What if I win Mackenzie?"

"No, no, no," Justin said. "We're a team. My team. You guys are just backup. You're just—"

"We're the guarantee," Sam said. "We get it. We just want to make sure you're not going to make us do the deed, too."

"What if I—we, the three of us—" Frog pointed to his buddies "—what if we choose the wrong fork?" His brows rose. "Daisy's fork?"

"That's just not going to happen," Justin said. "I have a sixth sense about these things."

"No, you don't," Suz said. "Even I know you don't believe in those things. You've said so a hundred times. In fact, this whole race, the only reason you're participating in it is that you believe it's a bunch of hokum."

"True," Justin conceded.

"It's just a charity event in which you're determined to beat out the Donovans," Suz said. "Which is all very noble except that my sister's heart is at stake. What will happen if you pick Daisy's lane? Just because you don't believe in the legend doesn't mean everybody else in Bridesmaids Creek doesn't. Very strange things happen on that road, and there's a reason those superstitions have come to pass. You've heard the saying, where's there's smoke, there's fire?" She studied Justin. "For every action, there's a reaction. It would be a bad reaction if you end up as Daisy's trophy."

"Won't happen."

"Because you think it's dumb. Because you don't believe," Suz argued. "In that case, I'll just take my sister's place."

"Hey!" Frog exclaimed. "Suz on one side, Daisy on the other side? Perforce the road not taken?" He looked distinctly uncomfortable. "In that case, I'll kneecap Justin."

Justin sighed, ignoring Frog's outburst. "That would work, Suz. You're a Hawthorne. Technically, you're single, a never-married bachelorette. It would work." He shook his head. "Anyway, it's not that I don't believe. I'm a participant, a bystander, new to this town. I don't have to embrace everything. I just play along."

Mackenzie walked in, and just the sight of her made Justin smile. "What are you guys doing?" she asked.

"Justin's trying to weasel," Suz said. "Who's watching the babies?"

"Jade and her mom came over," Mackenzie said, glancing around. "If you're going to play cards, you're welcome to do it at the house." She looked at Justin, and it felt like someone hit him with a bag of rocks.

He was in love with this woman.

"Are you being a weasel about something?" Mackenzie asked.

"I don't think so," he said. "We're trying to figure out how to win this race and stay inside the rules."

"He's sandbagging the race by having these three doofs run with him," Suz explained. "That way, he's inoculated from the whole wedding-in-thirty-days issue of the run, but he gets to be the big hero, too."

Mackenzie met Justin's gaze. "The way the Best Man's Fork run works is that one man makes a run to find a woman with whom he's truly in love. If he picks the right path and she's waiting at the end of the race for him, they're meant to be together. If he picks the road with no woman at the end, he might as well just keep on running."

Justin laughed. "I like my way better. The purpose is to win this thing, right? I don't want to win Daisy. So you're going to be on the other side. These three guys are going to run with me."

"On account of Justin's wonky leg," Suz explained. "Here's the thing he's not saying about this whole deal. Justin doesn't believe in the legend, but he wants to give it a trial run, you might say. Just in case it's true. But no one will ever know who is meant to be with you—or Daisy—because there'll be four runners. So basically it's just a charity run on a pretty day."

Mackenzie smiled. "Sounds fair to me."

Justin perked up. "Really?"

"Yeah. Let's do it Justin's way. No matter what happens, we win." She glanced at Justin. "Although you realize you're taking a terrible chance, Justin. You could end up married in thirty days. To Daisy. Fifty-fifty chance."

"Nope." He shook his head. "That's the good part about these goofs running with me. The curse will land on one of them. Probably Sam."

"Hey!" Squint sat up. "Who said it would be a curse?"

"I'm going up to the house to talk to Jade," Sam said. "She hasn't been around in a while, and I think she might have a little thing for me and is trying not to show it."

He departed. Justin glanced at Suz and Mackenzie. "Does she have a thing for Sam?"

"I doubt it very seriously." Suz stretched. "None of the four of you are long-timers here. Big *S*'s on your foreheads that stand for short-timers." She got up and whacked Frog lightly on the arm. "I'm going to be at that race. And if you run down the road where Daisy is, you might as well just keep on running, Rodriguez. Because you won't like what you get from Crazy Daisy."

She went out the door.

"Wow," Frog said. "Your sister scares me a little. In a good way. Pretty sure I like it."

Justin had had enough. He took Mackenzie's arm and pulled her outside, walking her away from the house. "Since it's about time to milk the cows—"

"We don't have dairy cows."

"Since it's about time to get up and drink our morning coffee," Justin said, "can you spare five minutes before you have to get back to the babies?"

"Maybe. Why?" Mackenzie asked.

"Mainly I want to make out with you." He pulled her into his arms, kissing her long and slow and deep. Sighed when she wrapped her arms around him, inhaled the sweet perfume of her hair and the softness of her skin.

"Suz says you're trying to rig the game your way," Mackenzie said.

"She's right. Every game has a better way to win it, you know. I'm not going to let the Donovans win."

"What's it to you?"

"What's it to me? I think BC's starting to weave its spell around me, that's what. And I happen to know a beautiful woman I feel like slaying dragons for."

"Very romantic." She cuddled up to him. She felt like part of his own body, his own breath. Justin closed his eyes, felt her trace his lips with her fingertips.

"So, listen. How does this end, when I win?" Justin asked.

Mackenzie smiled. "When you win, the Donovans slink off to figure out their next move. It's the never-ending chess game."

"I mean me and you. I try not to make too many moves on you, because of a thousand different reasons, not the least of which is you're the boss lady and everything else, although I think I'm past that. But how does this end?"

"Everything else?" She studied him. "What does that mean?"

"You've got the ex-husband trying to sue you, et cetera, et cetera, and being a general pain in the ass." Justin didn't stop himself when his hands somehow wandered down to her waist. "I guess I've figured you might not be interested in a—"

She kissed him. "Win the race. Then we'll find out how this ends."

Chapter Eighteen

The day of the race dawned clear and beautiful; the sun warming everything in its path with rich, soft rays. Justin felt good about today. Really good.

It was a town-saving kind of day.

His knee felt great. In fact, he felt like a warrior of old, like he could ride bulls until the moon came up again.

"Hey, stud," Daisy said, flouncing past him when he came out of the bunkhouse.

Trouble was up, and she was wearing a smile. "Hello, Daisy," he said cautiously. "Isn't there a rule about how the runner and the prospective bride shouldn't see each other the day of the race?"

She shrugged one dainty shoulder, tossed her bronze locks. "Rules were made to be broken, weren't they? And you're a rebel, right? That's what they say around the rodeo circuit, anyway." She went off, banged on the kitchen door and was allowed entrance. Justin hung back, deciding to delay his morning coffee and muffin with the babies—and of course their sweet mother.

Nothing good could come of seeing the woman he loved with the woman who intended to sabotage her on the big day.

Daisy had no idea they were intending to slip Mackenzie into the opposite fork. A decoy, as it were.

History was about to be made in BC.

Justin checked his watch. Two hours before he gathered up his team, put on his running shoes and got ready to prove everybody in Bridesmaids Creek wrong.

There was no such thing as a charmed and lucky road.

No such thing as a creek with mystic powers.

All there was was hard work. Determination. And a desire to win.

That was how you made magic.

"Good morning, Mackenzie," Daisy said with a smile that somehow grated on Mackenzie's nerves right off the bat. "How are the babies?"

"The girls are fine. They're just down for a nap." Mackenzie glanced at the baby monitor to make sure she'd switched it on. The girls had gotten into a routine that was almost regular, no easy feat with four of them. Somehow they seemed to have an intuition about each other. When one was upset, they all got upset. Happiness seemed to settle over them as a general mood, as well.

They'd come a long way.

"So today's the big race." Daisy looked at her. "It's like being crowned the king and queen of homecoming, only this is for real."

Mackenzie looked at her. "Whatever." She went to wash up the baby bottles in the sink.

Daisy cocked her head. "You seem very unconcerned about Justin running the Best Man's Fork. I'm the prize, you know."

"Daisy, there isn't a magic spell on earth strong enough to get Justin anywhere near an altar that you're standing at."

Daisy laughed. "You're sure?"

"Positive." She checked the pound cake and the level

on the tea, her mind on what she needed to leave behind for Jade and Betty's comfort. "Justin sees this as a charity function. The legend eludes him."

"That's because he's not from here. He doesn't understand how this town works."

"He's got a pretty fair idea." And he'd returned. Mackenzie smiled.

"You seem awfully confident."

"Look." Mackenzie turned to face Daisy just as Justin came in the back door. "Let me spell this out for you. You and your father and your gang can do anything you want to do to me, but you can't take the thing from me that I love most. You can't take my children, and you can't change who I am. You can talk about the man who died at our haunted house—"

"Was murdered," Daisy inserted.

"Never proven," Mackenzie snapped. "You can spread all the gossip and lies you want, and I'm still going to wake up every day being the same old Mackenzie Hawthorne my parents raised me to be. Which is more than you can take, because that's exactly what you're missing. Your spirit is damaged."

"Excuse me," Justin said. "I was going to grab a piece of that pound cake and maybe some coffee." He looked at Daisy. "Shame you picked me to be your runner. I'm really slow. Did anybody tell you they used to call me Turtle in high school?"

"What I heard," Daisy said, "is that you once ran a mile in under four minutes just to prove you could."

Mackenzie smiled at Justin. "I'll cut you some cake and get you some coffee. 'Bye, Daisy."

"I didn't come by just to talk," Daisy said. "I came by to let you know that there's going to be a tea after the race at The Wedding Diner. Held in our honor by Madame Matchmaker and Monsieur Unmatchmaker."

"I thought they were getting divorced," Mackenzie said.

"They are," Daisy said.

"Because your father ruined their marriage, the way the Donovans ruin everything."

"How is it our fault if Monsieur Unmatchmaker couldn't manage his finances?" Daisy asked. "Dad didn't have to loan him money."

"I'm sure he didn't." Mackenzie placed the cake and coffee in front of Justin.

To her absolute shock, he swept her into his lap, kissing her thoroughly.

"Wow," Mackenzie murmured.

"Um," Daisy said, "what the hell is that?"

"Collecting my prize early," Justin said.

Daisy's jaw dropped. "Are you two…an item?"

Mackenzie looked at Justin.

"Are we an item?" he asked.

"Do you want to be an item?" Mackenzie asked.

"Hey," Daisy said. "I want a different runner! You're out," she told Justin. "I'm going down right now to tell Jane Chatham and Cosette that I'm choosing a new guy to run the race."

She went out the door in a huff.

"Uh-oh. Look what you did," Mackenzie said.

"Couldn't help it." He kissed her again, this time longer.

"Guess you don't have to run today," Mackenzie said.

"Guess I don't."

"Which means I don't have to be waiting in the Fork to sabotage Daisy."

"It was such a great plan," Justin said. His hands stole up to her waist so he could tuck her closer against him.

"It was a great plan. But now that neither of us have

to be at the race, we have time to do something else."
Mackenzie touched his cheek, nibbled his lip, tried not
to inhale him.

"Did you have something in mind?"

"I most certainly do."

"I was hoping you'd say that," Justin said.

MAKING LOVE TO Mackenzie was better than running a
charity race for sure. It was sweet kisses and soft skin
and gentle heat that grew into a fire he had no desire to
control. Justin stared up at the ceiling while Mackenzie
slept beside him, feeling satisfied for maybe the first time
in his life.

All the old feelings of rebellion were gone. And they'd
started to be erased in this house, with this woman, with
her children.

Felt like the family he'd always wanted.

Not that he didn't love his family, but a man wanted
his own—and this was the one he hoped to put down
roots with.

If Mackenzie would have him.

She got up to dress, and he let his eyes roam wildly,
drinking in every bit of smooth naked skin he could. Wondered if he could drag her back into bed before the babies awakened.

He heard a baby cry and banging at the back door at
the same time. Time to get up.

"I'll get the baby," he said.

"Thanks." She kissed him and hurried down the hall.

There were excited voices coming from the kitchen.
"Sounds like something fun is happening down there,"
he told the babies, who were gazing around, riled by
Hope's crying, wondering if they should join the chorus.

He picked Hope up, calmed her and then heard footsteps flying down the hall.

Mackenzie burst into the nursery. "Suz is in town and she's going to hobble Daisy for life because Daisy chose Frog—Rodriguez—to run in your place. Suz told Jade that Daisy will never walk in high heels again when she gets through with her."

Justin shook his head and resumed changing Hope's diaper. "Young lady, you have a firebrand of an aunt."

"I have to go into town." Mackenzie hurried off.

"Which means I need to go into town to keep your mother out of trouble. Would you girls like to go into town?"

"This is all my fault," he heard Mackenzie mutter.

"Your fault how?"

"Because I kissed you in front of Daisy. She decided to cut her losses."

"Hey!" Justin laughed. "I resent that. I kissed you."

"And I liked it," Mackenzie called from the other room. "But now my sister is going to turn Daisy into a pretzel."

He didn't doubt that at all. "But Frog and Suz don't have anything going on, do they?"

"No, but that won't stop Suz and Daisy. Daisy thought she was going to be homecoming queen, but Suz won. It's bad blood."

"Let's pack the girls up and let them watch their first Bridesmaids Creek brawl. Think we could make a legend about that?"

Mackenzie hurried into the nursery.

"I'll watch them," Jade called. "By the way, I can hear every word over the baby monitor. I feel a bit like a creeper. And I like the idea of a Bridesmaids Creek brawl."

"I don't want my little sister fighting over a man." Mackenzie looked at Justin. "I've got to stop her."

"That I agree with," Jade called. "People will just say that bad things happen at the Hawthorne place."

Mackenzie gasped. "She's right."

There was a lot at stake, even if he couldn't grasp the whole concept of the underlying currents. "Do we even know if Frog agreed to take my place?"

"He did," Jade said, coming into the room. "I hope you guys are decent. I didn't want to keep listening over the monitor. Feels so third wheel."

Mackenzie hugged her. "You're never third wheel. You're family."

"Go. Just hurry." Jade waved them on. "Your sister's been spring-loaded ever since Daisy started flirting with Frog. It's really weird, because I never saw Suz get giddy over a guy."

"That's true. This is serious." Mackenzie hugged Jade and grabbed Justin's hand. "You're sure you don't mind going with me?"

"Mind?" Justin smiled, feeling like a king with Mackenzie's hand in his. "I wouldn't miss it for the world."

JUSTIN REALIZED HOW serious Bridesmaids Creek was about their social events when he saw that at least half the town had shown up at Best Man's Fork, expecting a race of some type.

What they got instead was an all-out vigorous debate between Suz and Daisy, with Rodriguez clearly the focal point of the discussion. Somehow that got other ladies and gentlemen involved, and the next thing he knew, even Cosette and Philippe were standing on opposite sides of the road that branched off into the fork where the victims— or bachelors, depending on how one looked at it—went off on the adventure of a lifetime.

"The Road Not Taken," by Robert Frost. Deep stuff this town lived by.

And it got a little deeper when Suz jumped on Daisy and dragged her by her long dark hair to the ground.

"Oh, no!" Before he could stop her, Mackenzie jumped into the fray, and then it was on. He looked at Frog, whose boots seemed glued to the ground. A hundred people either yelled insults or rolled in the dirt, engaged in some kind of combat. The sheriff and his men watched from the sidelines, and Robert Donovan complained loudly to the sheriff about his daughter's handling at Suz's hands, despite the fact that Mackenzie was working as hard as she could to drag her off.

"Are you going to do something?" Justin asked Frog.

Rodriguez shrugged. "Personally, girl-on-girl conflict is something a man probably wants to avoid. It's a no-win situation, or haven't you heard?"

"That's nice." Justin waded in, separated Suz and Daisy. "What the hell is wrong with you two?"

"I've wanted to tear you up for years," Suz said. "You just remember that, Daisy Donovan."

Daisy flounced off, straight to Frog.

Like a frog wanting out of a skillet, Frog took off. Squint and Sam looked at Justin.

"Are you going to help me separate the rest of these people?" Justin demanded.

"Not our battle," Squint said.

"Seems to be some kind of bad feelings in the general population around here," Sam said.

It wasn't his battle. Why did he feel so responsible?

Because he hadn't wanted to run. Hadn't believed in what the town believed in, what mattered to them—the legend that really covered up the last bits of hope they had that their town was going to survive.

It was falling apart.

Mackenzie ran to Suz. "Are you all right?"

Of course she was all right. Daisy was tough, but Suz was tougher. Daisy was sporting a fat lip and a scratch across a cheek, from what he could see at a distance, while Suz looked ready to go another round.

"I'm fine," Suz snapped. "It's just time someone taught Daisy Donovan a lesson, and her father, too."

That was all true. Even someone who was new to town could tell that the Donovans made consistent trouble for everyone. Even the haunted house might not ever rise from the ashes of the past.

Justin looked at the people scrabbling and arguing with each other all along the road—neighbors and friends who loved each other, when the Donovans weren't yanking everybody's chain and stealing their dreams—and took a deep breath.

"I'll run!" he yelled.

Chapter Nineteen

Mackenzie gasped at Justin's pronouncement. Everyone within earshot quit arguing and battling, which made the rest of the people take a break to find out what was happening.

"You can't run," Mackenzie said. "You have a bad knee."

"It's fine."

No way was she allowing this to happen. If he thought for one second he was going to run with Daisy standing at the other end of Best Man's Fork, she was going to go all Suz on him. Well, not physically, of course, but definitely she was going to give him a piece of her mind.

"Not to me, it's not fine," Mackenzie said, glaring at him.

Now that someone else's annoyance was front and center, everybody grouped around to hear every word.

"I'll do the run," Justin said, holding her gaze with his, "if Mackenzie's at the end of the race."

Jane Chatham came to the front of the group, clearly in her official position as marshal and rules enforcer. "Typically it's a bachelorette who—"

"Mackenzie's single," Justin said.

"No, Justin," Mackenzie said. "If you pick the wrong road—"

"I know, I know, keep running because the charm's broken, and we won't get married in thirty days, and I might as well be cast out of society because I'll never marry." He grinned. "Did I sum it up?"

"Well, you're pretty close," Mackenzie said, "because I don't want to lose you this soon."

He grinned. "I have a feeling it'll be fine."

"It's supposed to be my run," Daisy complained loudly. "I ask for the right to put in a champion."

"A champion?" Cosette wrinkled her nose, checked the papers Jane held. "Is that in the rules?"

"I choose Carson Dare, Dig Bailey, Clint Shanahan, Red Holmes and Gabriel Conyers to run as my champions, as I'm obviously being thrown over here," Daisy announced loudly, and the entire crowd gasped.

Mackenzie glanced over at the five men in black jackets, boots and blue jeans. Of course the purpose of Daisy's plan was to keep Justin from winning. Any of those men could outrun Justin, even if he claimed his leg was whole now. "You just can't stand for anyone to be happy, can you, Daisy Donovan?"

"I'm very happy." Daisy smiled at her. "And since it's a charity race, I'll donate five thousand dollars to the charity of the winner's choice."

"Even the haunted house fund?" Justin demanded.

The crowd went totally silent.

"Sure. I don't care. One good cause is the same as another," Daisy said. "There won't ever be a haunted house, but I understand the Hawthorne ranch is underwater these days."

Mackenzie shook her head. "Actually, we're in a good place. Thanks."

"We'll see." She glanced at Suz. "Neither one of you makes any money. It can't go on forever."

Those were words straight from Robert Donovan's mouth. Justin smiled. "So, are we doing this thing or not?"

"Justin," Mackenzie said, "I really wish you wouldn't do this."

"You just go pick your side of the road." Justin winked at her. "I'll be right there."

"I don't get to pick," Mackenzie said a little desperately. "The sheriff takes the lady in his truck to the finish line. She draws a straw to determine which side she takes."

"It's okay." He kissed her. "I'll find you."

"I wish you wouldn't do this." What terrified her most was what Daisy's band of jacket-wearing rowdies would do once they got past the view of the people. The forks wound through forest and brush-lined trails. It was a five-mile run, with no shortcuts. The sheriff and Cosette and Jane had driven it several times to check the distance and condition of the road. "I don't like it."

Sam, Squint and Frog stepped up to the line. "We'll run with him," Sam said.

"We're a team," Frog said.

"Like to keep things even," Squint said, glaring at Daisy's gang.

"There's five of them and four of you," Suz said. "Are you just itching to get a beatdown?"

Frog grinned. "We kind of thought the fight was weighted toward our side."

"Very funny," Dig Bailey said.

"All right, then," Cosette said. "The rules have been agreed upon—the game begins. Everyone who wants to be at the finish line will pay the race fund five dollars, no charge for anyone under twelve years of age! Monsieur Unmatchmaker, will you please fire the starting gun?"

Philippe grinned at his wife. "I'm honored. Let's get ready to run!" he yelled, excited to be chosen.

"When's the last time one of these races was held?" Justin asked Mackenzie.

"When my ex ran it," Mackenzie said. "Although he didn't really run it so much as walk it. And he didn't get to the right lane."

"He quit," Suz interjected. "He had a blister on his heel. It wasn't a race so much as a walk."

Justin looked at Mackenzie. "So history is indeed being made today."

She grinned at him. "Actually, history is being made because there's never been a race like this one. The rules are completely changed."

"You just remember that there's never been a race like this one," Justin said, kissing her.

"How are you going to run in boots?"

He smiled. "You just get in the sheriff's truck. The people want a battle, and a battle they're going to get."

JUSTIN WASN'T STUPID. He'd known when he and Mackenzie headed down here that there was going to be a race, and no man attended a race without a decent pair of running shoes. He'd tossed those in his truck, and he'd also tossed in a T-shirt.

"That's what you're running in?" Squint demanded, eyeing his jeans as the intrepid three pulled on extreme running gear. Their truck was parked beside his, providing perfect cover for their costume change.

"Yeah. I'm fine," Justin said.

Frog eyed him doubtfully. Reached over and lightly pounded his leg, scoffing in disgust. "You're still wearing that leg brace. Your leg isn't any better at all!"

"My leg is better," Justin said. "The doc said my knee would take a couple more weeks to fully heal the tear."

"That's just great," Sam said. "You can't run wearing a leg brace."

"I can run."

"Sure, Peg Leg." Frog's tone was total disgust. "You realize that if you take that brace off, your leg is frozen for a few days. You have to do therapy and crap to get the tendons and muscles and stuff back to normal. So you can't take that brace off because it won't do any good."

"I wasn't planning on taking it off," Justin said.

"Great," Squint said. "We're backing up Hopalong Cassidy. For five miles through forest and bush."

"Here's the deal," Frog said. "We've got your back. We're a team. So you run like hell and never look back, no matter what you hear behind you."

"What are you going to do?" Justin asked. They looked like they were getting ready for some kind of reconnaissance mission, all in black and camo. This was clearly just another mission to them.

"Just planning on keeping things honest," Sam said. "We're quite familiar with the way nonbeneficial things can happen in competitive times."

"Remember," Squint said. "No looking back. Very critical to your success. You've heard about Lot's wife and the saltshaker?"

Justin forbore a sigh and eyed his stalwart companions. "I really appreciate you guys stepping up on my behalf."

"Nah," Frog said. "It's not about you. It's about the boss lady."

Justin smiled. "Yes, it is."

MACKENZIE WAS NERVOUS as she rode with the sheriff. Not nervous. Apprehensive.

Maybe Justin was right—maybe this whole legend thing was dumb.

Except it wasn't. Cosette, Jane and Jane's husband had been busy taking money for tickets. Most of the town had turned out, since this wasn't an event that happened often and no one wanted to be left out. It was good for the town, it was good for the people and hopefully it would be good for her and her family.

The amazing thing was that Justin had been game to do it.

"I think you like that cowboy," Sheriff Dennis said.

"I wouldn't do this if I didn't." Maybe that's why she was apprehensive—it really, really mattered to her which lane Justin chose.

"I guess we should have all known from how the race went down with Tommy that he was a mistake," Dennis said.

"It's hard for me to regret anything because of my daughters."

Sheriff Dennis smiled. "I'd feel the same way. By the way, I heard through the proverbial grapevine that Tommy was dumped. His little girlfriend went off to greener pastures."

Mackenzie shook her head. "Somehow it doesn't matter anymore."

"True love," Sheriff Dennis said happily, parking the truck near the end of the thick woods where the paths converged again. "You know, whoever dreamed this race up was a genius. We should hold one every six months just on principle."

"You know very well who thought it up," Mackenzie said. "Cosette, Philippe, Jane, her husband and you."

Sheriff Dennis laughed. "You have to build a town from something. This was as good as anything. And we started this thirty years ago. How would you know?"

"Because I remember my parents talking about it,"

Mackenzie said softly. "They always said they were going to try it out one day."

Sheriff Dennis patted her hand. "They'll be tickled that their daughter is getting to do it right this time." He pulled out two straws, then hid them in his beefy palms. "Pick. You either want the right side or the left side of the road. East or west, there can only be one." He extended his hands to Mackenzie. "Choose wisely, Mackenzie. I've always thought of you as a daughter. This time I want you to be happy."

Her hand hovered over his. "What made you dream up the idea of Best Man's Fork?"

"There's a best man at every wedding, isn't there?" He looked at her, his eyes twinkling. "The spotlight can't always be on the bride and groom. Guys want to get married more than you ladies think we do. And we want a big deal made of it, too!"

Mackenzie smiled. "That one." She tapped his left hand, and he opened it.

She stared at the straw in his hand. If she hadn't known better, she would have thought it sparkled. Twinkled.

"I'll be leaving you right here," Sheriff Dennis said. "Good luck, Mackenzie."

She got out. "Thanks."

"You know the drill. That right there is your path. In a few minutes, there'll be all kinds of people swarming the finish line, anxious to see if Justin chooses the right road. Have you got faith in your cowboy?"

She closed the truck door and waved goodbye. Set out for the lane she'd chosen. There was no need to answer Sheriff Dennis's rhetorical question; they both knew she did or she wouldn't be waiting here for him.

Sheriff Dennis drove away. Mackenzie pulled out her cell phone and called Jade.

"Hello?"

"How are the girls?"

"They're darling! Mom and I are having a blast. Where are you?"

"At the finish line."

"Already?" Jade gasped. "It's going to go very different this time, you know. This time it's going to be—"

"Oof," Mackenzie said as something knocked her to the ground. Her phone flew, shattering when it hit a rock.

"Daisy Donovan! What was that for?" Mackenzie sat up and glared at Daisy, who looked proud of her handiwork. "Do not make me kick your butt today!"

She jumped to her feet.

"I'm not missing out on my chance," Daisy said. "You've already had your turn. Now move."

"Move?" Mackenzie frowned. "I'm not going anywhere."

"Yes, you are. Either you get in that other lane, or I'm going to make you wish you had!"

Mackenzie raised a brow. "What are you doing?"

"I'm going to be right here when Justin arrives." Daisy pointed to the other lane. "Go."

"Why don't you go to that side?"

"Because I know this whole gig is a bunch of hooey. Either the sheriff told you which side to choose or you just called your position in to someone."

"I was checking on the babies," Mackenzie said, disgusted.

"And giving her a coded location so that she could call one of the three dunces to clue Justin in on which road to take." Daisy pointed again. "Go, or you'll regret making me lose my temper."

"Daisy, you're never going to learn. Has your scheming ever gotten you anything you wanted?"

"We'll know soon enough."

"Justin isn't going to marry you."

"He may not marry you, either. But at least I'll have the charmed legend on my side."

Mackenzie sighed. "You realize that's about as good as believing in Santa Claus."

"Which I do. He was a saint, thanks. You know, that's part of your problem, Mackenzie Hawthorne—you're not a romantic."

"And you are?" Mackenzie could feel her brows elevate involuntarily. "Daisy, this is dumb. If you want this lane so badly, you can have it."

"Good. Because I really didn't want to have to knock you out and hide you in the bushes."

There was no point in arguing with Daisy. She'd always wanted what everyone else had; nothing was going to change now. She was Suz's age, still young, but as tough as Suz could be, Daisy could be tougher. It was as if she missed a key part of her soul that most humans had that made them compassionate.

"I thought you had a thing for Frog," Mackenzie said.

"Just flirting, nothing serious," Daisy said. "Move along."

"Just flirting?" Poor Frog might have actually thought Daisy cared about him. "What about Squint? Are you just flirting with him, too?"

Something strange came over Daisy's face. "Don't talk to me about Squint. He thinks he's special."

"So he turned you down?"

"He did not turn me down." Daisy's gaze slid away. "He said he isn't available for anything resembling dating, a relationship or even friendship."

"Ouch." Mackenzie hadn't meant to say it, and once the word was out of her mouth, Daisy glowered at her.

"Get over there, and when Justin sweeps me off my feet, you accept your just desserts. You've had this coming to you for a long time." Daisy stalked around a rock, dusted it off and sat down. "Dad's going to make marrying me very lucrative for Justin."

"You live in a dream world where Daddy's money gets you what you want."

"And you live in a dream world where Daddy's money didn't. Get lost."

Mackenzie went to the other lane, a good thousand yards away, and decided she liked the way the sun dappled the trees and the light breeze touched the lane. There was a tall tree made for climbing, with a slab someone had hammered in it for a seat that rose just above the canopy. There also was a tree swing and a bench, so Mackenzie took the bench and made herself comfortable.

"What the hell are you doing?" Suz demanded, hidden by a clump of leafy bushes.

"I might ask you the same!"

"Don't look like you're talking to me," Suz instructed. "It would be frowned upon by the town busybodies. And Daisy is an epic tattletale." She looked at her sister with exasperation. "I heard the whole verbal squall. Why did you let Daisy push you around?"

"Because I don't care." Mackenzie scooted closer to the end of the bench so she could see Suz better. "She can do what she likes. It won't change my destiny."

"Well, that's serene of you. It was all I could do not to jump out of the bushes and perform major facial rearrangement on her. And your phone is totaled."

"I'll replace it. And I can handle Daisy. You've got to quit worrying. Back to why you're hanging out in the hedge?"

"Keeping Daisy kosher. I knew she'd pull something.

I've known her ever since she came to BC, and she's always been a brat." Suz grinned. "Just happens to be I'm a bigger brat."

Suz was no brat. She was an angel with a good heart. "You're my darling sister, and I love you."

"Well, I wasn't going to let my big sister sit here on the biggest day of her life by herself," Suz said impishly. "I've got a good mind to go over there and do something to Daisy."

They both hesitated as the roar of vehicles heading up the road came to them.

"It's on," Suz said. "You've had your last five minutes to reflect on life as a single woman."

Mackenzie smiled. "It may not happen that way."

"Of course it will. Don't be silly. Daisy wouldn't have been so desperate to fight you for it if the legend hadn't come true every single time. Now you just sit there and think blissful thoughts. Your happy ending is on the way. By the way, this race is going to be a long one. You might want to get a nap in so you're fresh for your prince."

"Okay, I'll bite. What have you been up to?"

"Not me." Suz's face was the picture of innocence. "A little birdie told me Justin's knee is still in a soft cast. So he won't be tearing up the finish line to get to you." She grinned. "But he will."

"What are you talking about?" Mackenzie was alarmed. She hadn't seen anything on his leg. Not even when they'd made love.

"Just telling you what the birdies tell me." Suz grinned. "I think it's sweet."

She fell in love with Justin that much more, helplessly, happily in love. "Where are you going?" Mackenzie peered over the leaves that folded over where her sister's face had been.

Silence.

"Suz?"

But Suz was gone. Mackenzie smiled, thinking about how much she loved her sister. Nobody had helped her through her divorce and the ensuing bad times more than Suz.

She glanced over at Daisy to see what she was doing. No shock, she was combing her hair, primping in a mirror. Her long brown locks shone in the sun, her shapely, tanned legs daintily stretched in front of her in a skirt short enough to cause male heart failure.

While I'm wearing capri jeans, a sleeveless blouse and flat tennies, my hair in a ponytail.

It didn't matter. She'd held Justin in her arms. Even though he hadn't said the words, she knew he loved her.

She certainly was in love with him.

Mackenzie heard a squeal and commotion, and she glanced at Daisy again. Suz leaped on Daisy with a burlap bag, stuffing her in it before Ty carted her, struggling, to his truck bed and put her in it as if she were nothing more than a hay bale. He waved at Mackenzie; then he and Suz hopped in the truck and drove away.

Maybe it was cheating. Technically it was breaking the rules. Certainly she'd raised her sister to be more genteel and ladylike than to pin someone down and stuff them into a sack.

One day she'd return the favor for Suz. The very thought made her smile, and now that she was alone at the finish line of Best Man's Fork, Mackenzie suddenly felt very, very happy. In love.

As if this was the moment she'd been waiting for all her life.

Chapter Twenty

"Ready, set, go!" Cosette yelled and Philippe fired the starting gun, which brought a cheer from the crowd anxious to see Justin start the race.

He waved at everyone and took off at what he hoped was an impressive pace. His buddies had disappeared.

Which was fine with him. "I've got this," he muttered and headed to the fork. He didn't even hesitate; he already knew which way he was going.

He chose the left side of the fork, and a cheer went up from the crowd who'd gathered at the starting line. Justin couldn't say that this was something he'd ever imagined he'd be doing, but he was having a ton of fun. He felt like a warrior of some kind, a troubadour of old, going off to win his lady.

Which no doubt was exactly how Bridesmaids Creek intended a man to feel. Part of the fairy-tale charm and all that. Kind of silly, but if this was the way things were done here, he'd play along.

At the one-mile marker, the race monitor waved at him, offered him a water bottle, which Justin accepted, heading off without resting, determined to make a good showing.

At the one-and-a-half-mile marker—so designated by a giant heart-shaped sign posted on a tree—Justin was joined by the five doorknobs.

Daisy's gang set a pace behind him without saying a word. "More the merrier," he muttered and kept going.

They surrounded him at the two-mile marker, not touching him, but pacing along, in back and in front of him.

Annoying but not important. He had a job to do.

"Nice day, huh, fellows?" he said, just to be friendly, and then he ignored them as he tried to dismiss the fact that his knee was beginning to protest the treatment it was receiving.

Daisy's gang changed position, two on either side and one in the back. What the hell, maybe they figured they no longer needed a leader. He knew exactly where he was going, after all.

At the two-and-a-half-mile marker—another big heart-shaped sign—a commotion broke out behind him. Justin kept moving, not looking back, but his companions on either side of him did, and suddenly all hell broke loose.

Then silence.

"Don't look back, remember," he muttered and kept on going.

He ran alone after that, his thoughts busy with Mackenzie and the babies and how great it was going to feel when she told him yes. What man didn't think of the woman he loved telling him she wanted to be his wife?

He stopped dead in his tracks.

He'd *never* thought of it. Yet suddenly he couldn't *stop* thinking about it.

"Holy cow, there *is* something in the air around here." He glanced around, studying the thick foliage on either side of him. His shoes were dusty from the dirt road and his leg ached—he was far from his rodeo shape. The air was completely silent but for the occasional birdcall— mockingbird, for sure—and the sun beat down on him.

Some sixth sense or maybe even some of Bridesmaids Creek's enchantment pushed him into the woods. He crunched through tall grass and ground cover, beat back branches that rarely had experienced human contact until he got to the other road.

This was right. It was a rebel move, but he was playing a game with folks who were known to make the rules to suit themselves.

At the end of this road would be the woman of his dreams. That was how the legend went.

He ran like he'd never run before.

JUSTIN NEARLY HAD heart failure when he saw the final race monitor a hundred yards from the finish line, because Mackenzie wasn't there. His spirits sank. He looked wildly past the monitor, barely heard the greeting offered to him and crossed the tape at the finish line, bent over to gasp for air.

He could not believe he'd picked the wrong road. He hung his head. What the hell—it was a dumb charity race. He'd made the town some money, felt like he was a new-found son they were trying to weave into the fabric of their town.

It would all work out. He'd still ask Mackenzie to marry him, and hopefully she would say yes.

She might be a little tangled up because of that business with her ex being a loser at the race and the legend not working out too well for her that first time, but he could get her past that. Somehow.

He'd just have to convince her how much he wanted to be with her and the girls, forever.

"Hi," he heard at his elbow, and Justin stood straight up. Stared into his gorgeous lady's eyes, felt the mysterious wonder of Bridesmaids Creek fill him, changing him forever.

"Mackenzie!" He swept her into his arms. "Will you marry me?"

She laughed, and it sounded like pure joy to him. "Yes! Yes, of course. I would love to be your wife."

"I'm sorry." Justin took a deep breath. "I meant to ask you more romantically with flowers, a ring, maybe some hot sex to convince you I'm the only man for you."

"That was all pretty romantic." She kissed him, and it *was* the happiest moment of his life. Justin held Mackenzie in his arms, hardly believing how perfect his world had suddenly become.

"You were supposed to be at the finish line, weren't you? I thought I'd taken the wrong road." He ate her up with his eyes, wondering if he could get her to a wedding ceremony fast enough to suit him.

"I had to get the girls." She smiled up at him, and he saw Jade and Betty with the stroller of babies waiting under a shady tree. "The babies wanted to see you win."

"I'm a dad," he said. "I'm going to be a father to four beautiful little girls! I'm going to have four beautiful daughters and a gorgeous wife!" He laughed, hugging Mackenzie to him, his whole world opening up in a new way he'd waited his entire life to feel. Justin held Mackenzie, basking in the cheers from the townspeople who realized they were about to get their fondest wish, a wedding to attend.

"I love you, Mackenzie Hawthorne. The best thing that ever happened to me was the day Ty sent me to your ranch. I'm the luckiest man in the world."

Mackenzie laughed. "I love you, too," she said, "welcome home."

Justin grinned, reveling in the most magical, heavenly

moment of his life. How had this happened to him? How had he gotten the woman of his dreams, and the family he'd always hoped he'd one day have? He looked at the smiling faces of the people around them, felt their joy as they shared this amazing moment with them. It didn't matter how the fairy tale had happened. All that mattered was Mackenzie and the daughters he loved with all his heart.

He was home at last.

Epilogue

"So what about the haunted house?" Ty asked Justin on a day that was so beautiful Justin didn't think he'd ever known a better one. Of course most of the beauty that was in his life now was thanks to Mackenzie and her babies. He grumbled, slightly nervous as Ty situated his jacket and tie, having never been a groom before, only the man running in the Best Man's Fork race just last week.

It had been worth everything he had to see the smile on Mackenzie's face when he'd chosen the right path.

He allowed Ty to stuff a pocket square in his jacket, a useless detail he felt was unnecessary for the casual wedding he and Mackenzie wanted, but Ty was a stickler for details. "Mackenzie says the haunted house is part of Bridesmaids Creek. Now that there's some confusion about whether folks really want it reopened or not—"

"Hogwash," Ty said. "That was just stuff Daisy stirred up."

True, but Justin had done his part, which was rescuing fair maidens, all five of them. Actually, they'd rescued him. Now he was going to enjoy life in their world. "Mackenzie says it's a battle she's going to let Suz handle at this point. She says if anyone can corral Daisy, it's Suz." Mackenzie had also said that her time would now be completely taken up by making love to him, and haunted houses would have to take a backseat to that.

Which made him very, very happy.

"I don't like it," Ty grumbled. "No one else has any good ideas on how to save BC. That was my best one."

"It's fine, old buddy. You did your part. You can relax now." He slapped Ty on the back. "I want to thank you for telling me about Mackenzie's fake dating ad, by the way. Madame Matchmaker better watch out for you, obviously."

Ty laughed, pleased with himself. "It wasn't fake. I just never let it go live. And that's the last thing you're dragging out of me. I can't give up all my trade secrets."

They went downstairs and made a path to the altar. Justin was amazed by how many people had arrived to see their wedding, but then he realized he shouldn't be—this was BC. Everybody was always going to be in everybody's business—which was something that no longer worried him.

"Now I just need my bride," Justin said, and on cue the three-piece orchestra of two violins and a harp began playing and the guests swiveled their heads to look for the bride.

Suz came down the aisle first, sassy in a short pink dress, unable to resist squashing Ty on the toe with her high heel before she took her place at the altar.

"What was that for?" Ty asked Justin.

"I think you're in the doghouse for not fixing her up, too." But Justin couldn't worry about his buddy right now, because Mackenzie came around the corner, escorted by Sheriff Dennis, and Justin's heart felt like it was going to explode with joy. The babies were wheeled in a white carriage hung with pretty pink-and-white bows to the edge of the altar so they could have a front-row seat, and a happy sigh went up from the guests.

Mackenzie stood beside him, a short veil gracing her midlength faint pink wedding gown, her smile all for him.

"You're beautiful," he said. "The happiest moment in my life was watching you and the babies come down that aisle." He took her hand and kissed it, and the guests sighed again. "I love you so much."

"I love you," Mackenzie said. "I do, and my girls do, too. We all do."

"Yeah," Suz whispered. "Welcome to our family."

Okay, so maybe most sisters-in-law wouldn't butt in, but it was Suz, and, frankly, he was delighted to hear that she thought he was a good thing for her sister. Mackenzie laughed and he smiled; the babies laid almost perfectly still in their pram, fussed over by Cosette and Jane, and Justin's life became a rodeo of a different kind. Bigger, better, happier.

Which was a completely happy ending for a rebel cowboy.

And if he thought he heard Ty mutter, "One down, three to go," he paid no attention to his buddy at all.

It was a most enchanted day in Bridesmaids Creek.

* * * * *

Watch for the next book in Tina Leonard's
BRIDESMAIDS CREEK *miniseries,*
THE SEAL'S HOLIDAY BABIES,
available November 2014
only from Harlequin American Romance!

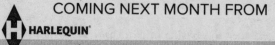

COMING NEXT MONTH FROM

H HARLEQUIN®

American Romance®

Available August 5, 2014

#1509 TRUE BLUE COWBOY
The Cash Brothers
by Marin Thomas
Beth Richards decides to celebrate her divorce by picking
up a cowboy, and gorgeous Mack Cash is perfect. After an
incredible night, Mack wants to get to know the real Beth—not
an easy task when he wakes up alone.

#1510 THE TEXAN'S LITTLE SECRET
Texas Rodeo Barons
by Barbara White Daille
When her dad has an accident, Carly Baron returns home—and
faces her former lover Luke Nobel, manager of the Barons'
Texas ranch. Their attraction is rekindled, but single dad Luke is
certain Carly is hiding something.

#1511 A COWBOY'S HEART
Hitting Rocks Cowboys
by Rebecca Winters
Liz Henson and Connor Bannock have always kept their
distance because of their feuding families. Now they're
traveling together in close quarters to the National Finals
Rodeo...and finally giving in to their forbidden attraction!

#1512 THE COWBOY MEETS HIS MATCH
Fatherhood
by Roxann Delaney
As teenagers, Jake Canfield and Erin Walker fell in love. Now,
even though Erin realizes her feelings for Jake have never
waned, he's a reminder of the baby she gave up for adoption....

**YOU CAN FIND MORE INFORMATION ON UPCOMING HARLEQUIN® TITLES,
FREE EXCERPTS AND MORE AT WWW.HARLEQUIN.COM.**

HARCNM0714

REQUEST YOUR FREE BOOKS!
2 FREE NOVELS PLUS 2 FREE GIFTS!

HARLEQUIN®

American ★ Romance®

LOVE, HOME & HAPPINESS

YES! Please send me 2 FREE Harlequin® American Romance® novels and my 2 FREE gifts (gifts are worth about $10). After receiving them, if I don't wish to receive any more books, I can return the shipping statement marked "cancel." If I don't cancel, I will receive 4 brand-new novels every month and be billed just $4.74 per book in the U.S. or $5.24 per book in Canada. That's a savings of at least 14% off the cover price! It's quite a bargain! Shipping and handling is just 50¢ per book in the U.S. and 75¢ per book in Canada.* I understand that accepting the 2 free books and gifts places me under no obligation to buy anything. I can always return a shipment and cancel at any time. Even if I never buy another book, the two free books and gifts are mine to keep forever.

154/354 HDN F4YN

Name	(PLEASE PRINT)

Address	Apt. #

City	State/Prov.	Zip/Postal Code

Signature (if under 18, a parent or guardian must sign)

Mail to the Harlequin® Reader Service:
IN U.S.A.: P.O. Box 1867, Buffalo, NY 14240-1867
IN CANADA: P.O. Box 609, Fort Erie, Ontario L2A 5X3

Want to try two free books from another line?
Call 1-800-873-8635 or visit www.ReaderService.com.

* Terms and prices subject to change without notice. Prices do not include applicable taxes. Sales tax applicable in N.Y. Canadian residents will be charged applicable taxes. Offer not valid in Quebec. This offer is limited to one order per household. Not valid for current subscribers to Harlequin American Romance books. All orders subject to credit approval. Credit or debit balances in a customer's account(s) may be offset by any other outstanding balance owed by or to the customer. Please allow 4 to 6 weeks for delivery. Offer available while quantities last.

Your Privacy—The Harlequin® Reader Service is committed to protecting your privacy. Our Privacy Policy is available online at www.ReaderService.com or upon request from the Harlequin Reader Service.

We make a portion of our mailing list available to reputable third parties that offer products we believe may interest you. If you prefer that we not exchange your name with third parties, or if you wish to clarify or modify your communication preferences, please visit us at www.ReaderService.com/consumerschoice or write to us at Harlequin Reader Service Preference Service, P.O. Box 9062, Buffalo, NY 14269. Include your complete name and address.

HAR13R

SPECIAL EXCERPT FROM

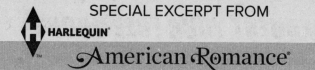

HARLEQUIN

American Romance

*Harlequin American Romance is excited to introduce a
new six-book continuity—**TEXAS RODEO BARONS!**
Read the following excerpt from*
THE TEXAN'S LITTLE SECRET, *where Carly Baron
confronts her past in the form of cowboy Luke Nobel…*

The cowboy standing in the barn doorway started toward
the truck. He wore a battered Stetson, the wide brim
shading most of his face, but no matter how much she tried
to convince herself this was just any old cowhand striding
toward her, she couldn't believe the lie.

He halted within arm's reach of her driver's door, his
eyes seeming to pin her into her seat. "Carly Baron," he
said. "At last."

"Luke." She forced a grin. "Isn't this flattering. Seems
like you were just waiting for the chance to run into me."

"I figured it was bound to happen once Brock said you'd
come home again. But when I never caught sight of you,
I started to wonder if he'd been hitting the pain pills too
hard."

"I'm not home again. I'm just visiting."

"The helpful daughter."

"That's me." She shoved open the door and a double
dose of attitude made her stand straight in front of him.
He stared back without saying a word. Let him look all he
wanted. One touch, though, and she'd deck him.

"It's been a long time."

"And you've come a long way." If he picked up on the

added meaning behind her words, he didn't show it. "I hear you're ranch manager now. Daddy's right-hand man. You finally landed the job you'd always wanted."

He got that message, all right. His jaw hardened. "You think that's what it was all about? I wanted to get to your daddy through you?"

"I said that to you then, and you didn't argue. But it looks like you found a way without me, after all."

"Funny. By now, I would have thought you'd grown up some."

"I expected you'd have grown beyond working for my daddy."

"A man's gotta have a job," he said mildly. "And I guess none of us knows what the future has in store."

"I'm not concerned about the future, only in what's happening today. *And* in making sure not to repeat the past."

"Yeah. Well, what's happening in my world today includes managing this ranch. I'd better get back to it."

"That's what Daddy pays you for," she said.

He touched the brim of his Stetson. "See you around."

Not if I can help it.

Look for THE TEXAN'S LITTLE SECRET
by Barbara White Daille, the first installment in the
TEXAS RODEO BARONS *miniseries.*
Available August 2014
wherever books and ebooks are sold.